JOY CHILDS

Marguerite Dolby
56 Whitecross Gardens
Derby
Friday September 10th 1993

HALL — DERBY

To my husband, Rob, and my mother-in-law,
Irene, with love and thanks.

DOROTHY

A story of intrigue, divided loyalties – and love – set amid
the wild, but beautiful Derbyshire Peak District in Tudor
times.

Dorothy Vernon's name has become synonymous with
her elopement from the ancestral home which she later
inherited. It was above all to her a bid for happiness
against the odds, not least of which was the opposition of
her formidable father, 'the King of the Peak'. But its
consequences were more far-reaching than either she or
her husband, John Manners, could have envisaged.
Friendship for the young pair, and support for their
marriage, came from the most unexpected quarters, and
when the captive Mary Queen of Scots arrived in
Derbyshire, it was not only Dorothy who derived strength
from the rock-like assurance of John against the
prevailing uncertainties of the time ...

This novel of Dorothy's life and love presents new light
on an old romantic piece of history, placing her and
Haddon Hall, her home, at the very heart of the era in
which she lived.

First published in Great Britain 1984
Hardback Edition
ISBN 0 7090 1661 1

Robert Hale Limited
Clerkenwell House
Clerkenwell Green
London EC1R 0HT

Paperback Edition 1988

Published by J. H. Hall & Sons Limited
Siddals Road, Derby DE1 2PZ

ISBN 0 946404 66 6

Photoset in North Wales by
Derek Doyle & Associates, Mold, Clwyd
Printed in Great Britain by
J. H. Hall & Sons Limited,Derby
Bound by Backhurst & Taylor Limited, Nottingham

Contents

The photographs are from 'Scenes from Sixteenth Century Haddon'
performed by the Peacock Players in the Lower Courtyard
during June 1987

'Sir George who of ye Vernons was ye last
That held those goodlie lands, from whom they past
By two Coheires out of the Vernon's name
(For which great Talbott was ye more to blame),
Sir George I say of who yet manie speak
For great houskeepinge termed King oth' Peak ...'

The Rhymed Chronicle of John Harestaffe
Derbyshire, 1615

Author's Note

The usual story about Dorothy Vernon tells us that she eloped from Haddon Hall in Derbyshire on the night of her sister's wedding in about 1563.

Or did she? Apparently, the household accounts for Haddon Hall show that Margaret Vernon was married in the first half of 1558 and from the end of that year until 1564, there is a curious gap in these accounts.

However, it is generally supposed that Dorothy was married in the fifth year of Elizabeth I's reign, 1563. The romantic circumstances surrounding this survived through an oral tradition in the area around Haddon which passed from one generation to the next for almost 300 years before it eventually found its way into print in 1822. The first published story about Dorothy, written by Allan Cunningham, contains certain details which have for me the ring of truth and I have therefore included these in this novel.

Another factual clue to this 'mystery' comes, I believe, from the lines already quoted: through her alliance, Vernon lands passed out of the family name, *For which great Talbott was ye more to blame*. George Talbot, 6th Earl of Shrewsbury, was known in Elizabethan Derbyshire as 'Great Talbot' or 'the Great Earl'. He lived very much at the centre of this turbulent era of English history and, as will be seen in the novel, had more than a vested interest in Dorothy's marriage.

I wish gratefully to acknowledge the help I have received in writing this book from the following:

William Adams, *The Gem of the Peak*.

Allan Cunningham, *Traditional Tales of the English and Scottish Peasantry*.

M. Paul Dare, *Aylestone Manor and Church*.

Derbyshire Archaeological Society, *Derbyshire Archaeological Journal*, vols. 7, 8, 10, 22 and 30.

Peter Draper, *History of the House of Stanley*.

David N. Durant, *Bess of Hardwick*.

Antonia Fraser, *Mary Queen of Scots*.

Historical Manuscripts Commission, *Calendar of Rutland Manuscripts, Calendar of Salisbury Manuscripts*.

Joseph Hunter, *Hallamshire*.

R.H. Kinvig, *The Isle of Man: A Social, Cultural and Political History*.

Janetta Manners, *Haddon Hall*.

P. McGrath, *Papists and Puritans under Elizabeth I*.

John Nichols, *History of Leicestershire*.

S. Rayner, *The History and Antiquities of Haddon Hall*.

Sheffield City Libraries, *Dorothy Vernon's Elopement: Tale or Tradition?*

G. le Blanc Smith, *Haddon, the Manor, the Hall, its Lords and Traditions*.

John Timbs and Alexander Gunn, *Abbeys, Castles and Great Halls of England and Wales*.

F. Earle Willis, *A History of the Parish of Uffington*.

Prologue

As the wind hushed through the moonlit night, stirring lacy branch patterns on the window of Dorothy's chamber, the shrill hoot of an owl suddenly disturbed the air.

Dorothy sped to the open window, her heart pounding, and peering down she saw a tall figure in the shadows below.

Her bundle of belongings soon joined him. Now it was her turn. The moment of escape! She must be quick. Success depended on speed. She could hardly contain her tears as she embraced her two servants and said she would send for them – eventually.

Then Joan tied part of the long cord firmly around her waist and after Alice had tested it and nodded, Dorothy clambered as quietly as possible through the window. Behind her the cord was held fast by her waiting-women. She eased herself round to face the wall, her feet searching desperately for a foothold. Scrape, scrape, their sounds seemed to echo menacingly through the night. A deadly fear smote her, almost panic. What if someone heard? And came to investigate? Then the noise of revelry in the hall rang clearly all around her once more. She clutched the rope with all her strength.

"Now!" she whispered to her servants, and little by little they let out more rope as her feet inched their way down the wall ... lower ... lower ... then a rush of sheer delight as she was suddenly lifted into the strong pair of arms reaching up for her.

At last her feet touched the ground. Swiftly, John untied the rope around her, and after a silent wave of thanks to Alice and Joan, the lovers were running, through the woods a little way, down the slope towards the river bank and skirting below Haddon Hall towards the footbridge. The merry-making still reached them in an ever-augmenting din. Across the bridge, two more dark figures emerged from behind the trees, John's men, awaiting them there with horses.

"Farewell, fair Haddon," said John. "We shall return and

bless this night!''

With triumph and relief, Dorothy kissed him tenderly as he helped her into her saddle. No more words were needed. These were their moments of greatest danger, yet in their joy they both felt a sense of perfect peace.

And so the gallop through the moonlight began, the two servants turning south towards Rowsley and Matlock, to create a false trail to Wiverton. And Dorothy and John towards Bakewell, Sheffield and the north. So close did the happy pair ride off together that their shadows merged into one to follow, lengthening, behind them in their tracks and soon the spire of Bakewell Church came into view, seeming to beckon them towards it.

Almost five years to the month since my mother was laid to rest there, reflected Dorothy. Dear lady mother, all this began when we lost you ...

PART I: 1558

'Remember me when I am gone away,
Gone far away into the silent land.'

Christina Rossetti

DOROTHY VERNON

This portrait is an authentic likeness of Dorothy
when a girl. It is copied by permission from an old oil painting
in possession of His Grace The Duke of Rutland.

The engraving of Dorothy Vernon is taken from 'Doll:'
A Dream of Haddon Hall by J. R. Muddock, published in 1880 by
John Heyward of London, and is reproduced by courtesy of
Derby Local Studies Library

Bakewell Church

ONE

Dorothy walked slowly down the nave of Bakewell Church with tears stinging her eyes. Looking up, she saw the maidens' funeral garlands suspended from the arches. The most recent one had been placed there during her last visit – in memory of a thirteen year old girl. Thirteen, the same age as herself! She had been deeply moved at the time and suddenly made fully aware of her own great wish to lead a long and happy life.

And she had built up a vivid dream of her future, in which she was walking in bright sunlight by the river Wye at Haddon, arm in arm with her husband, who was young, tall and bearded, though she could not see his face. There were children too, sons and a little girl playing by the narrow stone footbridge as she and her older sister, Margaret, had done so often during their childhood.

The two sisters now placed their own flower garlands, of primroses and violets, on their beloved mother's grave and there they knelt, the sound of their prayers drifting out of the Vernon Chapel into the farthest corners of the church. This place seemed such a peaceful haven to Dorothy compared with the bustling activity at home and she had ridden here frequently since the grievous loss of her mother in March, two months ago.

"I can sense her presence," whispered Dorothy. "It is as though she is with us yet, in mind at least."

"She is here, Dorothy, I know she is. And it is very comforting," replied Margaret.

Rising gradually to her feet, Margaret turned then to her betrothed, Sir Thomas Stanley, and spoke with her characteristic composure, "Thomas, I cannot go straight back to Haddon. I would ride freely over this wide open country just once more before I leave here as your wife."

He understood that. And so did Alice Shepney, the sisters' old nurse and chaperon.

"Come," she said, taking Margaret's arm. "Let us ride further over your father's lands. Lands which will one day be yours!" She looked kindly from Margaret to Dorothy and then with a knowledgeable air at Thomas. "One thing we can be sure of – Mistress Margaret will never stray too far."

Mistress Dorothy, however, glancing swiftly away from Alice, had secret doubts whether the same could be said of her!

As they rode beyond Bakewell, Margaret raced on ahead of her companions, her cloak and waist-length hair streaming out behind her. Only then did Dorothy imagine herself in Margaret's place – leaving this countryside she loved for a long time, perhaps never to return –

Away with such unpleasant thoughts!

She saw Thomas spur his horse and gallop after Margaret. He called back to her. She looked appealingly at Alice.

"Oh, off you go!" said the nurse indulgently. "And mind you don't be too long."

The hood of Dorothy's cloak fell away as she gathered speed to catch up with Thomas and Margaret and she too felt the exhilaration of the wind in her flowing auburn hair. She was glad to be young, glad to be alive and with the promise of her whole life before her.

By the time they reached Ashford-in-the-Water, a village just inside the neighbouring Chatsworth estates, the usually delicate pink bloom of Dorothy's cheeks had flushed into a healthy glow.

They slowed to a leisurely pace, walking their horses by the banks of the river Wye.

"If we turn back now, I think there'll be time for a game of bowls before supper," she said enthusiastically.

"Bowls? I do not recall making plans to play bowls with you, Mistress Doll," teased Thomas.

"Well, I intend to play," she retorted with a smile, "and you're very welcome to join me."

His merry eyes twinkled at her. Thomas had just discovered that when she smiled in her gentle, but lively, way Dorothy was growing up into one of the most beautiful girls he had ever seen.

But it was graceful Margaret whom he loved. She seemed serious now, which turned his own handsome expression to one of concern.

"What is it, my love?" he asked.

"Dorothy is right. We should return now," she said quickly.

Thomas was intrigued. "Why this sudden urgency? Has something happened here? Something unpleasant perhaps?"

"Aye, something I would rather forget," she replied emphatically. "But all of a sudden I remembered where we are …"

"Near Galley-acre!" burst in Dorothy.

"What in the world is Galley-acre?"

"*Gallows* Acre is its real name, Thomas," she explained. "'Tis a field near here." She shuddered and her face grew narrow and pinched under his renewed gaze. "A man, one of the Haddon tenants, was once hanged there by order of our lord father and without a lawful trial."

"Rough justice!" mused Thomas. "He is well named 'the King of the Peak' then in these parts."

"Nay, Sir George Vernon is so named for his wondrous hospitality," cried Dorothy ruefully. "Not for his strictness in other matters …"

She would have poured on, regaling Thomas with further examples of her father's strictness, but for the cogent "Hush!" which then came from Margaret.

Respecting this, Dorothy said to Thomas more slowly, "He must never know it was I who told you this."

"And he never shall, you have my word."

"Then I think this conversation were better ended," ventured Margaret. "I would treasure my memories of today."

Thomas grinned, then shrugged his shoulders. They rode back in silence at first, their track never far from the river. Ash, hazel and birch trees in places lined its banks and honeysuckle climbing wild along some overhanging branches melted them with its sweet fragrance.

"Though our lives may change, some things endure," smiled Margaret to Dorothy. "The land, and the plants and trees."

"And the river," said Dorothy, thinking of her dream. With

all the sudden insecurity in her life, it was good to know of, enduring things. Her youthful high spirit re-asserted itself, lifting the other two and soon the air was filled again with their merry chatter.

Nearing Bakewell, they found Alice enjoying the shade under a small clump of trees.

"Back so soon?" she pretended to grumble. "Doesn't an old nursery crone deserve a longer rest?"

Thomas dismounted, laughing, and handed his horse's rein to Margaret. "Come on, old crone," he quipped, helping Alice back onto her 'nag'.

And then they resumed their journey to Haddon, talking affably about Thomas and Margaret's wedding, to be held soon at Whitsuntide, of the many guests who would arrive, and of the bridal pair's future life together on the Isle of Man, which Thomas was to govern for the Earl of Derby, his father.

Dorothy felt a contented glow to see her sister so happy.

But with only their father left now to settle her own future, she wondered wistfully what lay ahead for her.

On the morning of Margaret's wedding day, guests moved like bright birds around the gardens of Haddon Hall.

Dorothy strolled happily onto the third garden terrace, where she soon caught sight of the Talbot family. What joy it was to be with people such as these! Tiny spots of sunlight glinted on the fine stuff of their clothes, bathing her friends in an aura of welcoming silver stars. She was heading straight towards them, when she was suddenly stopped in her tracks.

"Mistress Dorothy, what a perfect day for the wedding!"

This stock remark came from the bridegroom's sister-in-law, Margaret Clifford. Dorothy agreed with her, hurriedly, having already exchanged many such greetings with passing guests and wishing now only to reach the Talbots.

"Don't you wish this was your day? Don't you feel jealous of your sister?" the lady went on.

One of these words, spoken so lightly, pierced the girl's vulnerability and she repeated it, ill concealing her annoyance. "*Jealous?* No, my lady. Why should I be?" She checked at a warning look from her father, who stood nearby, then tried to explain more calmly, "My sister has always been very close to me and I shall miss her sadly."

Perhaps you are the one who is jealous, she thought angrily as she moved on. Dorothy had been watching Margaret Clifford with much curiosity during the last few days, for it was the first time she had been so near anyone with even a remote claim to the English throne. Yet in this young cousin of the Queen, who was at present held in very high favour, she could sense great unhappiness, even fear. And the frequent quarrels between this lady and her husband, Thomas's older brother, were plain for all to see. Dorothy felt glad that the closest she herself would ever get to a royal title was 'Princess of the Peak' as Thomas had teasingly called her.

Her father would probably reprove her for discourtesy. Well, what did she care! He could not accuse her of that towards any of his other guests.

Still fuming inwardly, Dorothy was so preoccupied that she almost collided with Lady Talbot.

"Oh, my lady, please forgive me," she apologised, her small hands gripping the lady's arm.

"Do not fret, my dear," replied Gertrude Talbot, slightly amused at the intensity of Dorothy's concern. "You look troubled. Can you tell me? Perhaps a walk down to this little bridge of yours might be good for you. The Countess will stay with the children."

Dorothy nodded, smiling gratefully at her. Although the old Earl of Shrewsbury and his heir, Lord Talbot, were away in the north, she had welcomed the rest of his family to Haddon with an abundance of enthusiasm.

She felt a great lightening of her mood as she went down to the next garden terrace with Lady Talbot and then began the steep descent to the footbridge. Dorothy could not explain why, but despite the considerable gap in their ages, she found this lady very companionable, as her mother had done. And as for Gertrude herself, she felt drawn to the girl and rather protective.

A cool, refreshing breeze met them when they stepped onto

the bridge and saw the sunlight shimmering on the fast-flowing water beneath them. This had always seemed a soothing place to Dorothy, hidden as it was by the trees on both sides and the sharp bend in the river.

"I feel much better already," she declared to her sympathetic companion. "A remark was made to me that I might be jealous of my sister. Me! I wish her nothing but happiness. Margaret is one of my dearest friends as well as my only sister ..."

"You seem a little angry with yourself also," noted Gertrude.

"I know," Dorothy pouted. "At the time I thought I was going to lose my temper. Twas wrong of me."

She relaxed again, feeling confident in the presence of Lady Gertrude. "If I do envy Margaret at all, it's because she has much of my lady mother's quiet dignity about her, whereas I cannot always control my emotions."

"Margaret has a more serious turn of mind than you, Dorothy. You must accept that," said Gertrude. "But there are five years between you, and by the time you reach her age, I expect you also will be more composed! You are very alike in some ways."

It was a much more hopeful Dorothy who, some minutes later, ascended the steps from the bridge. Enduring things, Margaret had spoken of. Did friendship endure?

"Please, God," she prayed silently, walking beside Gertrude, "let this one last."

Soon they were back with Countess Grace and the four young Talbot children.

"Mama, please may we see the dogs again?" insisted eight year old Francis, the eldest child.

"What, again!" grimaced Lady Gertrude.

At her request, Dorothy conducted them readily into the parlour, where they immediately renewed their acquaintance with the white Talbot dogs depicted on the ceiling, recalling an earlier marriage between their two families.

"Just like our Jack," commented Francis.

"And who is Jack?" asked Dorothy, amused.

"Our big white dog," came the reply. "He plays with us and lets us ride on his back. Would you like to meet him, Mistress

Dorothy?"

"You will do very soon," promised Gertrude, and exchanged a purposeful glance with the ageing Countess.

After the long-protracted midday meal, Dorothy repaired to her sister's chamber where, as she expected, she found Margaret looking placid and cheerful, even radiant in her own way. If the bride felt apprehensive about her marriage, she certainly gave no indication. And Dorothy did indeed envy the quiet assurance with which Margaret faced most situations. She wondered if, when she herself was eighteen, she really would meet life so calmly.

The young bride's body was cleansed with sweet herbs and her skin anointed with her favourite jasmine scent.

"How long before you sail to the Isle of Man?" asked Dorothy, helping Margaret into her chemise.

"Some time yet. We will go first to Thomas's estates at Winwick and then on to Lathom, his father's house."

"And we will see each other again soon? Otherwise I couldn't bear the loneliness."

Dorothy's eyes were brimming with tears.

"Of course we will," smiled Margaret. "Now, Doll, I have a gift for you to remember me by."

Margaret motioned to her maid to bring over a small box from the top of her clothes chest. When Dorothy opened this, her face filled with wonder at the exquisite golden rosary she lifted out.

"Thank you. It's beautiful!" she cried, hugging Margaret. "I will keep a lock of my lady mother's hair with this, so then I can remember my dearest mother and sister both at once."

Margaret released herself unobtrusively from Dorothy, as though trying to spare the girl further pain. But Dorothy, still clutching her sister's gift, wrapped her arms around the front of her own body.

"Now, now, Mistress Dorothy," clucked Alice. "Go to! We must prepare your sister to meet her bridegroom."

She marched Margaret across to the oval looking-glass, harrying her about lack of time, resembling even more an agitated hen. The bride remained unruffled, although she did steal a quick glance at Dorothy, now happily flapping her arms in imitation of Alice. Both sisters giggled. Their old nurse, it seemed, was another of those enduring things!

Later on, when the splendours of the nuptial mass and the wedding feast were over, Dorothy delighted the bride and groom with her gift to them, of silver goblets embossed with their initials.

Leaving them surrounded by well-wishers, she stepped lithely from the dais back to the body of the banqueting hall, which had now been cleared of benches and trestle boards. She cast an eye at her father and saw nothing untoward. Sir George mingled happily with his guests, though often through the moving lines of dancers, she glimpsed him with two in particular. One of these was Lady Cavendish, their neighbour from nearby Chatsworth, and the other a matron whom Dorothy did not recognise.

Driven solely by instinct, she sought the company of Gertrude Talbot.

"Who is the other lady talking to my father?" she enquired earnestly.

"That's Lady Port, my dear," smiled Gertrude. "She and Bess Cavendish are childhood friends. A coincidence, is it not, that both have been widowed recently for the second time?"

But instead of answering that, Dorothy plunged on to another question. "And that girl with them now, is she Lady Port's daughter?"

"Maud Longford? Yes. She is about Margaret's age. I heard talk that she hopes to marry some Earl's son."

Something made Dorothy look more closely at the sullen, dark-haired Maud and she could not understand why she should sense a familiar feeling in her: unhappiness, the same as that of Margaret Clifford.

And watching that deep conversation, Dorothy herself grew fearful. Gertrude's former words had at last penetrated her mind, with an effect of shock. "Both recently widowed for the second time." She thanked Gertrude for the information, smiling into her eyes, forgiving her. The lady had not *meant* to cause Dorothy further turmoil. But which of these widows was to marry her father? Dorothy had rushed to this conclusion of course, knowing him as she did, believing that she was preparing herself for the worst ...

The dancing and revelry were at their height when the bride left for her chamber. She was attended by several ladies, her sister amongst them, who were to help her get ready for bed. Margaret had been overjoyed with the feasting and congratulations, but as she stood, silent and night-robed, by the ornate nuptial bed over which the chaplain was making the sign of the cross, she smiled a little nervously at Dorothy.

It was not long before she and Thomas lay between the silk sheets together, Sir George drew the bed-curtains on them and they were left alone at last.

For Dorothy, now, the sudden temptation to flee from the festivities was almost irresistible. Her feelings of loss were once more assailing her, with potent force, and she was overcome with dismay. Clasping her tremulous hands together on the way back to the hall, she mumbled, tight-lipped, for permission to retire. Her father granted this and she bobbed him an unsteady curtsey. Once out of his view, she ran to her own chamber and then flung herself headlong on the bed and wept as she had not done since her mother's death.

This time her words of comfort came from Alice, who put her to bed as she had done when Dorothy was a small child. Eventually the girl passed into a fitful sleep, her memories of Margaret's wedding being blighted by the frequent sight of her father talking to Ladies Cavendish and Port.

A few days later, the two sisters clung to each other before Margaret departed from Haddon.

"I am so happy for you," Dorothy told the newly-married pair. But she was too young to hide her feelings. Her eyes told Thomas and Margaret Stanley how much she would miss them both.

"Farewell, little princess, till we meet again," said Thomas. "I'll look after my Lady Margaret well."

With Sir George she climbed up the spiral stairs to the top of the Peveril Tower and watched their progress across the Derbyshire countryside until they were tiny figures in the distance.

Dorothy lived much within herself during the following, long weeks at Haddon, seeking the refuge of the little bridge whenever she could. Sometimes she went there by way of the Nether Gate, passing under the old archway carved with her parents' initials, G.V. and M.V. for Sir George and Lady Margaret Vernon.

She could remember the day when her father had ordered these carvings to be made, only one of the happy childhood memories which now came back to her in the minutest detail.

The middle of June brought the promised invitation to visit the Countess of Shrewsbury and Lady Talbot at their Derbyshire residence, Wingfield Manor.

"I believe you will benefit from this visit, Dorothy," Sir George told her. "It'll do you good to be away from Haddon for a while, especially after the recent events here. We will go at the end of the month."

The time cannot come quickly enough for me, thought Dorothy, but made her voice reverent as she acknowledged his words.

TWO

Dorothy's spirits rose immediately when they came in sight of Wingfield Manor.

"So many hills to reach this place!" grumbled Sir George, then added with a clumsy gentleness, "But I'll grant you this much, Doll, its setting is very fair."

The manor house itself was situated on a low, steep hill, commanding an impressive view over the Ashover valley and, like Haddon Hall, it was built around two courtyards.

The clatter of horses' hooves announced the visitors' arrival with their servants in the outer court, where they were greeted by a confusion of scurrying stable boys, barking dogs and four excited children escaping from their nurse.

Lady Talbot appeared in the gateway, closely followed by Countess Grace.

"Welcome to Wingfield Manor," she said, a sentiment expressed repeatedly and with great enthusiasm by her lively offspring.

Dorothy embraced them all warmly once she had dismounted. Sir George responded with his usual courtesy, deferential if rather aloof, especially towards Gertrude Talbot. He liked the lady herself well enough. After all she was the well-loved wife of one of his closest associates and had been a good friend to his own wife, and now his daughter. The fact that she was also his kinswoman was something he preferred not to think of.

Absently, he patted his young godson, Gilbert, on the shoulder as the boy pointed insistently towards the gateway. A large white hound came bounding through to welcome them in his own exuberant way.

"And this, I suppose, is Jack," laughed Dorothy, bending to stroke him. "He certainly is very friendly!"

"He is one of the family," said Gertrude, "very gentle with the children and never happier than when he is with them. He guards them well!"

The Countess conducted Dorothy and her father to their rooms on the west side of the inner court.

"This is judged by many people to be the most beautiful part of the house," she explained.

"Thank you, my lady. You are most gracious," replied Sir George. "I am sure we shall be very comfortable here. I myself must return to Haddon within the week to look to my estates, but my daughter is anxious to remain with you and my Lady Talbot for a while, having been parted so very recently from both her mother and her sister."

"She may stay as long as you wish, Sir George."

A feeling of great delight washed over Dorothy. Now the loneliness of her immediate past seemed like a bad dream and neither fear nor pain could touch her again, for here she was happy and secure.

She smiled thankfully at them both, then turned to look out

over the hills.

"It is undoubtedly beautiful," she said.

Her happiness increased even more during the next few days, so that when the time came for Sir George to leave, she could not feel sad. Not when she was glowing with such new life. He bid her enjoy her stay at Wingfield and said that he would send for her.

As Dorothy watched him go, there was an urgent tugging at her gown.

"Dolophy, come quickly!" squeaked a little voice at her side.

She looked down to see three year old Mary, the youngest of the children.

"You may call me Doll, as my lord father does sometimes," she smiled, picking up the little girl. "That will be easier for you to say."

The child put her arms around Dorothy's neck and nestled closely to her.

"Well, I see there is a prior claim upon your company," laughed Gertrude. "I'll be in the still-room if you need me."

And away she went through the inner courtyard.

Dear lady, I shall always need you, thought Dorothy affectionately, and then found herself much in demand, jokingly reeling under the impact as the other three children came running up to her with Jack.

"Time for our rides," announced Gilbert noisily. "Come and watch us, Mistress Dorothy."

"Yes, *please* come," panted Katherine. "We've been longing to show you our rides."

Dorothy was more than willing to accept their invitation. And whose joy is greater, mine or theirs? she asked herself, while she and the children's nurse supervised their rides on the faithful Talbot dog's back.

The warm July days were passing so pleasantly that the girl lost all sense of time. Often she assisted Gertrude in the still-room, preparing various scents and lotions. With the children, accompanied as always by Jack, she played or walked in the gardens on the east side of the house, told them stories she remembered from her childhood, helped Gilbert with his reading and Katherine with her laboured attempts at embroidery.

"You are truly good with the children, Dorothy," said Gertrude to her as they relaxed in the gardens one afternoon. "They respond to you as well as they do to my brother John. Of all their uncles, he is by far their favourite."

Uncle John! The children were beside themselves with excitement at this mention of his name.

"When does he come to see us again?" Francis wanted to know.

"Oh, not until next week," smiled his mother.

"Do you have many brothers?" asked Dorothy.

"Yes, I have five. My eldest brother is of course the Earl of Rutland, then there is John Manners, the second eldest. My brothers are all great friends with each other and also with my lord husband."

"I wish I had brothers – and more sisters," sighed the girl.

Gertrude looked at her thoughtfully. Probing deeper that evening when she and Dorothy sat alone together, embroidering, she had occasion to ask, "Do you know that I'm your cousin?"

"No. No-one has ever mentioned that to me," replied Dorothy, bewildered.

"I thought not," said Gertrude a little sadly. Very carefully she helped herself to some more gold thread from the colourful pile on the cushioned seat beside her.

"But, lady, why?" cried Dorothy, her face suddenly lighting up. "You know I rejoice to hear such news."

Gertrude warmed to her, smiling in the firm, kind way she used with her children. "I cannot say for certain, Dorothy. Only that ... before you were born, your father and my uncle, Sir Richard Manners, were not on the friendliest of terms. You may not remember Sir Richard. He died when you were a small child. He was Sir George's stepfather and lived for some years at Tong Castle."

"I wonder if *that* is why my father has always been more attached to Haddon than to our Shropshire home," speculated Dorothy. She laid aside her needlework, being far too aflame now to concentrate. "My lady, the Vernons have been buried at Tong for generations and yet for my mother he chose Bakewell!"

"A departure from family tradition?" mused Gertrude. "Well, he has been Lord of Haddon since he was three years old."

"And John Manners is my cousin? And the Earl of Rutland?"

Dorothy was amazed. She looked forward to meeting her cousin ...

On a morning in late July, Dorothy was seated on the garden lawn, patiently allowing Katherine and Mary to practise dressing her hair, first of all with green ribbons and then with a net. Grimacing, she quickly removed this net which held her red-gold hair so that she could experience the freedom of letting it fall over her shoulders and down to her waist.

"Such beautiful hair, tis a pity to hide it with a net," said a deep voice behind her.

She turned round suddenly to find a dark-haired young man looking at her with startled interest.

John had approached with Gertrude and his two nephews. Immediately Dorothy could see the family resemblance between them, apart from the fact that he stood head and shoulders above the lady.

He's about the same age as Thomas! she thought with pleasure as she scrambled to her feet and curtsied. He was younger than she had expected, though still some ten years older than herself. To Dorothy, all young men in their early twenties were comparable to her handsome brother-in-law, and when she considered John Manners she found to her surprise that he compared extremely well.

His charm and ease of manner soon became apparent to her, as did his sheer enjoyment of romping with the children. Small wonder they so clearly loved him! In turn, he lifted the three younger ones high above his head and made them squeal with delight.

"Put me down, put me down now, Uncle," laughed Katherine. "Or else I'll pull your hair!"

"Oh, how I tremble! I am in great fear, my little lady," he said, setting her gently back on the ground and making a mock bow.

"My go now!" yelled Gilbert, pushing past his brother in his eagerness, which caused the indignant Francis to lunge at him determinedly.

"What, fighting again!" cried John, stepping quickly between them. His blue eyes flashed as he grinned wickedly from one to the other. "Methinks I must punish you for such unbecoming behaviour."

He then picked up a twig and brandished this at the two boys, who played up to him with suitable grunts and groans of pain.

"John! Be careful!" The warning tumbled from Dorothy's lips without her thinking. Her enjoyment of the banter swiftly turned to alarm as a snarling white dog suddenly launched himself at John and grabbed the twig in his mouth.

Instinctively, she ran towards John, her face betraying her great unease.

"Tis naught but a scratch, Mistress Dorothy," he smiled reassuringly at her, "but I thank you for your concern."

He took her hand in his and kissed it, so light and gentle a touch that she felt a shiver run through her. "Alas, that my visit here should necessarily be so brief," he added softly.

Then he whistled and the dog came bounding back, circling round both Dorothy and John, and on command he sat in front of John, offering him a paw in token of their friendship. This was gladly taken and then the children dissolved into laughter, their dearest uncle having clearly regained the loyal Jack's affection!

Dorothy and John also laughed. As he straightened up after letting go of Jack's paw, she watched him, full of admiration. Everything about John seemed good – and *strong*, she thought. Not just his build, but his voice and bearing. She could envy him his confidence, but to her, a young girl so alone and unsure of herself, his strength seemed very appealing. Alas, indeed, that his visit should be so short.

And though John left after only three days, homeward

bound for his Nottinghamshire manor, the impression which remained with Dorothy was both favourable and lasting.

July days passed into August. Countess Grace became ill and when, in the middle of the month, Dorothy's father sent for her she left her friends at Wingfield with a heavy heart.

For once in her life she did not wish to return to Haddon and the weather, cold and dank, did nothing to raise her spirits. Through a shroud of mist the grey stone walls of her home loomed up before her as she approached with her escort of servants.

When she reached the upper courtyard, Sir George himself was there to lift her down from her saddle. They greeted each other amicably enough, she thought, but still her sense of foreboding lingered. They went inside to the parlour. He sent for food, but she ate very little. Across the table they surveyed each other, sitting stiffly in their high-backed chairs.

"Lady Port and her daughter, Maud Longford, will be our guests from tomorrow," Sir George informed her in his matter-of-fact way. If that was no surprise to Dorothy, his next statement struck her like a thunderbolt. "Mistress Maud is to be your new stepmother."

For a long moment she stared at him in stunned silence. Then she astounded even herself with the vehemence of her reaction.

"No! No!" she screamed in a repetitive torrent, recalling vividly her impression of Maud on Margaret's wedding day.

"Oh yes," retorted Sir George icily. "You should know better than to question your father's decisions, my girl. If not, there are ways you can be taught! You will receive my guests with courtesy and a calm frame of mind."

"No! It's too soon … after my lady mother …"

He sprang up then from his seat, pushing his chair backwards so forcefully that it tipped over. "It was God's will that claimed your mother's life," he bellowed, "and dead wives can always be replaced!"

"My mother can *never* be replaced!" She burst into floods of tears.

Sir George rounded on her as if to strike her, then suddenly softened in spite of himself.

"Nay, Doll," he said, stroking her hair. "No doubt I spoke too sharp. Did you think that I should ever cease to love your lady mother now that she is dead, loving her so greatly as I did in her lifetime? But I have no son, Dorothy, to succeed to my estates. And I am old, although forty-four is not too old to beget a son! My wife-to-be is young and healthy. She may yet bear me one. And you, one day like Margaret you will be well married. Would you have me left entirely alone?"

"Oh no, father." She was sobbing more quietly now. But the miserable Maud! How could he even consider marrying her? Dorothy hoped she would be able to hide her resentment.

Haddon Hall in the autumn: the bronzes, dark greens, russets and coppery-reds of the trees on the thickly wooded hillside behind the manor house made a striking contrast with the pale grey of its limestone walls and turrets.

But down on the little bridge, Dorothy felt more despondent than ever. Her father and Maud Longford were married: Sir George and Lady *Maud* Vernon instead of the beloved Lady Margaret! Now those initials, G.V. and M.V. seemed to leap out and mock her when she passed under the old archway.

Another friend had died – Grace, Countess of Shrewsbury. Dorothy was beside herself with grief. Why was it that in this terrible year of change her friends and those she loved most were either dead or far away from her? There had been one brief and happy reunion with Thomas and Margaret before they sailed for the Isle of Man. Then she returned to emptiness and isolation – and her distress was even worse than she had feared.

Alice Shepney was now her sole confidante at Haddon and her presence was valued more than ever by her dejected young mistress. Often she joined Dorothy on the bridge, where she could listen to her and comfort her out of earshot and out of sight of the house.

"Alice, I shall never enjoy the same closeness and companionship with my Lady Maud which I had with my mother and sister," said Dorothy. "But at least now I know why she is so unhappy and I am sorry for her."

"Aye, she was forced to wed in order to please her family," said Alice tonelessly. "I believe she resents this marriage as much as you do."

"But he is more than twice her age! And against her will! If that is my father's idea of an arranged marriage, *I* will not be forced when the time comes," she cried bitterly, defying the knowledge that Sir George would expect her to accept his choice of husband for her without question, whether it pleased her or not.

In her mind she often heard again the voice of her sister saying, "My lady would not have forced me to accept." Lucky Margaret! Hers was arranged as a brilliant match between two powerful Catholic families, but the bridegroom himself was a decidedly attractive prospect. And it seemed to Dorothy that the spirit of her gentle mother lived on in this happy marriage which she had done so much to bring about. She was the only person who could soften the extremes of Sir George's formidable temper, and it would for ever be Dorothy's tragedy that Lady Margaret Vernon had died when her second daughter was still so young.

Down on the bridge, and in the daylight, Dorothy looked long at the river and dreamed her own special dream. She clung to it nowadays, for it soothed her. At times the sunlight reflected its golden length across the water and then she thought of her friends at Wingfield – the warm-hearted Lady Talbot, four lively, happy children playing with a large white dog, and a handsome, dark-haired young man who had charmed her during his short visit there.

But at night in the gloom and loneliness of her darkened chamber, the dream turned into a nightmare. The tall, young husband by the river suddenly shrivelled into a hunched figure and turned his face towards her. An old and ugly face! Night after night she awoke shivering and heard a voice screaming "No!" over and over again. The voice that she heard was her own.

When she was with Alice, they sometimes talked of who Sir George's choice of husband might be for her – when the time came.

"My father's new marriage came as a shock to me," she said, "and I'm sure the same will happen again regarding my own marriage."

"Please try not to disturb yourself about that, ladybird," soothed the nurse.

"I cannot help myself, Alice," cried Dorothy. "All I know is that he will choose a member of a rich Catholic family. One of the Derbyshire families perhaps, or one of my Vernon cousins. And how much say will my Lady Port have in the matter?"

Her hands gripped the top of the bridge. Lady Port, she had discovered, not only had great influence with Sir George, but was an even stricter Catholic than he was. She was also related to several leading Derbyshire families and her second husband, Sir John Port, had, like Dorothy's cousin, Henry Vernon of Sudbury, been responsible for burning a blind Derby girl called Joan Waste at the stake only two years before. And all because the girl chose to remain a Protestant! Since then, Dorothy had felt rather wary of cousin Henry.

"I am afraid of such strict Catholics," she affirmed. "If they were ever required to change their beliefs, even a little, and become more tolerant, would they?"

She doubted it.

Dorothy did not realize how soon her thoughts would be put to the test. But there were changes in the air which would deeply affect everyone.

Even in remote Derbyshire, the rumours were rife during that autumn of 1558. The Catholic Queen was dying. Who would be her heir? Her popular sister, Elizabeth, or her young Catholic cousin, Mary Queen of Scots? There were some who regarded the English princess as a bastard with no true right to the throne; there were others who eagerly awaited the prospect of her accession and the return of the Protestant faith.

In a friendlier moment between them, Dorothy had heard her father refer to Lady Cavendish's prolonged absence from Chatsworth. She was apparently living at Brentford, waiting upon events at Court.

Dorothy plucked up courage to ask him. "What will happen to the Church if the new Queen changes things again? What will happen to us?"

Sir George met her gaze directly. "The Vernons would not
welcome any changes, Dorothy, but we must be prepared to
expect them," he said. "Under the Tudors, there are some
subjects who are made of solid oak and others of willow, and
like the willow they bend with any wind of religious change.
Who knows what will happen? It would depend on the extent
of change, whether we are of oak or willow. Like many others,
my daughter, we wait upon events."

On 17th November, Queen Mary Tudor died and once the
news reached Derbyshire, it was acted upon without delay.
Dorothy awoke one morning to hear the sound of church bells
ringing, the bell of Haddon chapel in the foreground and those
of Bakewell and Rowsley in the distance.

The new reign had at last begun, and the bells helped spread
the message: long live Queen Elizabeth!

PART II: 1560-63

'But to see her was to love her,
Love but her and love for ever.'

Robert Burns

Musicians in Tudor costume at Haddon

THREE

"God's greetings, my Lady Countess."

"John! I am glad to see you."

In the crowded state apartments at Wingfield Manor, the new Countess of Shrewsbury forgot all formality as she received her brother's embrace.

But when he released her, Gertrude noticed immediately that John's gaze had wandered away from her and rested intently on the lovely young girl who stood beside her – and he could scarcely hide the effect of her beauty on him.

He bowed and the girl sank into a billowing curtsey.

"Why, Mistress Vernon," he said softly, "you have grown fairer than ever."

"Master Manners ..." Dorothy began, her face alight with pleasure.

He led her into a carefree conversation, relieved at the calm politeness of his own voice and that his powers of dissembling were sufficient to include Gertrude in a quick exchange of small talk while he delighted in the girl.

So this was the pretty child who had caught his eye on that visit to Wingfield over two years before? He had hoped he would see her again, amongst those invited guests who were now assembled to honour the new Earl and Countess.

And here she was, no longer a child! At fifteen, Dorothy had grown taller and glowed with bright health, her colouring enhanced even more by the gown of pale green which moulded itself against her slender, shapely body. A small cap of the same colour rested on the smooth auburn hair and her soft hazel eyes seemed even larger and more lustrous than before.

With reluctance John excused himself from her presence when he realised that the tall, thin figure of the Earl was beckoning to him across the room. The sudden change in Dorothy's expression did not escape him, however, as he saw her cast a troubled and furtive glance at the Earl's two dark-haired companions, one of them a well-built, middle-aged man with long hair and beard, and the other a small, neat young woman. It seemed to him as though, despite the girl's obvious happiness at receiving his attention, she reproached herself for being caught off her guard.

She smiled apologetically at John, then turned back to talk to his sister.

George Talbot, 6th Earl of Shrewsbury, stepped forward and welcomed his brother-in-law warmly.

"And how go matters at Court, Master John?" he asked. "I hear such reports about you Rutlands enjoying high favour with the Queen."

John grinned. "Then I suppose you have heard that my brother, Roger, has joined the royal household. And as for the Earl of Rutland, Her Majesty has appointed him Lord President of the North."

"A great honour. That was held as you know until recently by my lord father, God rest his soul."

"The Shrewsburys are still highly regarded, my Lord Earl," John reassured him. "Queen Elizabeth refers to you affectionately as her 'old man'!"

Shrewsbury chuckled. Although he had only succeeded to his title on the death of the old Earl in September, two months earlier, and was still in his thirties, his kindly but often serious countenance made him look older than his years.

"In the meantime, my lord," continued John, "let me congratulate you and my sister, the Countess, on the birth of your new daughter."

"Aye, another niece for you, John! We named her Grace after the late Countess, of course. We would have liked a third son, but mayhap next time. Sir George Vernon here tells me that he now has a fine grandson."

The Earl turned and introduced John to Dorothy's father and stepmother. The two men bowed formally, then Sir George eyed the younger man searchingly. Lady Maud allowed a slight smile to part her lips, but chose to remain silent and subdued.

"I trust your grandchild does well, sir," said John.

"Yes, thank you," Sir George responded, becoming visibly

more friendly since the subject was so dear to him. "He is named Henry and was born recently to my elder daughter, Lady Margaret Stanley.".

He looked meaningfully at his young wife, who merely bowed her head.

John would have liked to mention Sir George's younger daughter, but he resisted the impulse. He was not surprised to find, however, that Dorothy now occupied a high place in his thoughts.

He was aware of her at the banquet which followed in the adjoining hall, aware of her because, of the many voices around him, he could hear one voice which was higher and sweeter than the rest. Its owner sat further down the table, her small hands treating the rich array of cheer with such delicacy that John studied her, enraptured. The sound of girlish laughter bubbled forth at some remark passed by the Earl, who sat near her.

My Lord Earl, fain would I change places! John reflected, smiling.

But whenever John Manners contrived to be in Dorothy Vernon's company during the following days at Wingfield, he had mostly to be content with watching her and admiring what he saw – the sweet animation of her face, the graceful movements of her body and the quiet, courteous charm which she displayed towards everyone.

The girl seemed to be constantly chaperoned either by her grave stepmother or by his own sister, Gertrude, who walked affectionately arm in arm with her and was usually surrounded by her four eldest children with Jack. They at least were as lively and eager as ever for their Uncle John's company!

He noted the loving look which came into Dorothy's eyes when she held Gertrude's healthy, gurgling baby. "Grace," she murmured, "tis a beautiful name."

If ever she looks at *me* like that, thought John, what passion she will kindle!

Yet there was a disarming innocence in her manner, an unawakened air which aroused in him not so much desire as a strange new impulse to protect.

They both joined one of the Earl's hawking parties, but there she stayed close to her father, who seemed pleased to have her with him. Though they danced together, sang and played music, Dorothy and John were always within sight of many other people.

And even when he did manage to converse with her beyond the surface pleasantries, he found that her mind was far away on the Isle of Man, centred on a little boy whom she had never seen. A baby boy called Henry, the son of her beloved Thomas and Margaret. Her own nephew. How she yearned to see him!

It seemed appropriate that John's Talbot nephews and nieces should bring their closest moments together at Wingfield. Dorothy had donned her dark green cloak and briefly taken the air with Francis, Katherine and Mary. There was a touch of frost on this early November day and the thoughts of the log fire in the hall quickened their footsteps as they entered through the porch.

But just inside, Dorothy stood rooted to the spot, spellbound by the sweet and gentle strains of a lute accompanying the rich tenor voice of a man who sang round and true on every note. The voice she instantly recognized, the love-song she did not know, but so beautiful did she find it that tears glistened in her eyes.

Her murmur of appreciative delight met John when he finished his song. As she took off her cloak and laid it on a carved chair near the entrance, he motioned to her to sit beside him near the fire. The slight figure of Gilbert Talbot stood close to him on the other side and the white dog lay at his feet.

"Mistress Dorothy," he grinned, "I would teach this nephew of mine to play the lute correctly. But he will have none of it. Instead, he has the nerve to demand that *I* play to him!"

His clear blue eyes twinkled as he pinched the boy's cheek.

"That doesn't surprise me," smiled Dorothy. "I too demand that you play more."

Their eyes met then, in a look of lingering tenderness. We understand each other, they seemed to imply.

Her feet tapped in time to the music as John's elegant fingers plucked the strings. They sang together ballads and part-songs, with the four children joining in as best they could. Even Jack involved himself by emitting the occasional whine.

"We shall make more music next time we meet," said John, for he knew that she was leaving the next day.

"I shall look forward to that," she replied.

When the Vernons departed, Gertrude saw her brother disappear into the High Tower on the west side of the manor house. She had noticed too the deep seriousness which had of late replaced much of his usual banter. She decided to follow him up the spiral staircase to the top of the tower, where she encountered him staring out over the surrounding countryside, with a remote brooding look on his face.

"Why so pensive, John?" she asked sympathetically.

"I think you know already."

"Dorothy Vernon?"

"Aye." His gaze fixed firmly on the group of riders bound for Haddon. "By God's precious soul, I love her, Gertrude, and I think that she cares for me. Hardened soldier that I am, my mind is filled by a beautiful, sunny-haired girl. I tried to see her alone, but I was disappointed."

"Have a care, John!" remonstrated the Countess. "Above all things, you must guard her honour. She is little more than a child – a gentle, sensitive child and she has suffered much since her mother died. Even now she is more lonely and unhappy than she realizes."

"Then I would marry her and make her happy," he said determinedly. "If I should ask for her, would you use your influence with her father to aid me?"

"I do not think so," frowned Gertrude. "By all means, enjoy her friendship, but I would advise you to seek elsewhere for a wife."

He looked at her in amazement. "What are you trying to tell me, my lady?"

"That Dorothy's father may well refuse you, despite your noble birth and the royal blood in your veins. You probably know that he cares not for our family, but at this present time there are at least two other reasons."

"As far as I can see, he always treats you with the greatest courtesy," observed John.

"Polite platitudes!" she answered scornfully. "Yes, Sir George Vernon's courtesy towards me is always outwardly correct. He tolerates me, for after all I am a Talbot by marriage. But you still carry the name of Manners." She placed her hand then on her brother's arm. "John, although our uncle was Sir George's stepfather, his guardian as such was his own uncle, Sir John Vernon of Sudbury. I believe he is still very close to the Sudbury Vernons and may look there for Dorothy's husband."

The group of riders was receding rapidly into the distance. At Countess Gertrude's invitation, John descended from the tower with her and accompanied her to her private sitting-room, where they settled down comfortably in cushioned chairs.

"What are these other reasons?" he asked.

"Religion, for one," she said. "We are now committed Protestants, but the Vernons, although they attend the Church of England as required ..."

"Church Papists?"

"Yes. In their hearts they still cling to the old faith, hoping maybe for better times to come. Some of Lady Maud Vernon's kin don't even bother to conform outwardly."

"And that's why they're among the Derbyshire gentry who were not invited here by the new Earl and Countess?" mused John, leaning forward in his chair.

Gertrude nodded. "Lady Maud's widowed mother is one of these Catholic recusants. I fear the Government will instruct my Lord Earl to penalize them soon. He is not a cruel man, but he had little time for those who disobey Her Majesty's laws."

"My Lord Earl," repeated John proudly. "Already there are some in this county who call him the Great Earl!"

"And in this county, Sir George Vernon is second only to the Shrewsburys in terms of power," added Gertrude.

"And so?"

"That brings me to my second reason why he might object to you as his son-in-law." She too leaned forward now, moving nearer to the fire, and her face was pale as she went on:

"He has no son of his own, John. And until he has,

Dorothy's marriage is of the utmost importance to him, for she will inherit a considerable portion of his lands. Perhaps that is why he wavers over choosing her husband."

"But I would marry the girl for herself alone," said John. "Lands or not."

His sister shook her head. "Nay, she has several potential Catholic suitors within the Vernon family, then there is Lord Derby's youngest son ..."

"And what of Dorothy's feelings in all this? If only I could find out for certain!"

"I have no power to prevent you," sighed Gertrude.

"None at all," he assured her. "You say that Dorothy is sensitive. Well, surely if ours was a love-match, her father would not object?"

"But those who marry for love," she reminded him.

"Shall lead their lives in sorrow? I do not believe that, Gertrude," declared John, suddenly standing up. "But I do know that there can be no-one else for me. I thank you for you anxious endeavours to acquaint me with the situation. However, I think now that I shall be in the Earl's retinue when he visits Haddon next week, as he requested me. I have a mind to taste some of this famous hospitality of Sir George Vernon. After that I will go as a guest not bidden if necessary!"

"Then I can only ask that you be gentle with Mistress Dorothy – and discreet," said Gertrude.

"I promise you that, my Lady Countess," he smiled.

The Derbyshire countryside had never seemed so beautiful to John as they travelled towards Haddon. Golden hair made him think of golden colours, the shades of autumn, of coppers, reds and bronzes blending into the gold of leaves falling in the sunlight. The weather was mild for the time of year and the roads were still firm. In a few more weeks they would become impassable.

Dorothy stood beside her father to welcome their guests, and when he saw her smiling happily at him, John's ardour for her increased. He too felt happy, and strangely bewildered, no longer the self-assured young nobleman in favour at Court. Yet the Earl of Shrewsbury made no secret of the cordial friendship between himself and this brother-in-law of his, and the hospitality which John received from the Lord and Lady of Haddon was, as Gertrude had said "outwardly correct". But still he had not seen Dorothy alone.

His opportunity came most unexpectedly. A messenger had arrived at Haddon with bad tidings, causing Dorothy to keep to her room and Sir George to look haggard and drawn. Shrewsbury had made some brief explanation to John, then joined Sir George to continue their private business discussions. By chance John found himself left alone in the great chamber directly above the parlour, where he spent some time looking out over the gardens from the oriel window. A sudden movement caught his attention and then his heart leapt when he recognized the tiny figure on the steep steps by the fourth garden terrace. Her skirts billowed out as she ran quickly out of sight, but there was no mistaking that gleaming mass of hair. In a few moments he had descended from the great chamber and out through a narrow passage into the gardens.

Standing on the little bridge, Dorothy was too lost in thought to hear the footsteps behind her. But there, as she peered at her own reflection in the water, was the much taller one on her right hand side.

"Master Manners!" she gasped. "You find me unattended. If we should be seen ..."

"Never fear, Dorothy. Although these trees have lost most of their leaves, we are still well screened from the house."

She noted with trepidation that he had not used the word 'mistress' before her name, and John could see that she had clearly been weeping bitterly, although this in no way marred her youthful beauty.

He held a lock of the hair which fell about her shoulders, and bending his head, swiftly kissed it.

"Sir!" she exclaimed. "You presume too much."

"I wish I might presume more," he said.

"Please leave me. I would be alone."

"Why, then, do your eyes invite me to stay?"

Unable to hold back her tears any longer, she covered her

face with her hands. He took her in his arms and kissed away the tears, gently and without passion.

"Tis your nephew?" he enquired. "I heard so from the Earl. I am very sorry."

"Little Henry, dead," she sobbed. "Why do so many children die?" In her mind she pictured clearly the sorrowful faces of the bereaved parents.

"Your Thomas and Margaret are young," he consoled her. "They will have more children."

"Oh, I hope so. I hope and pray you are right."

A quality of calmness returned to her as she rested her head against him. Only then did Dorothy realize how comforting she found his presence and how, for the first time in an age, she also felt safe and protected.

"I am so glad you are here, John, so very glad," she whispered.

He responded by tightening his arms around her.

"I love you, Dorothy," he said quietly.

And beneath them, it seemed that the sparkling waters of the river Wye were dancing, making melody among the stones. A gentle breeze caressed the pair before whispering away through the trees. But the most musical sound to John Manners was the rustling of Dorothy's gown against the walls of the narrow bridge, as they stood there together in a tender embrace.

FOUR

February 6th in the third year of Elizabeth's reign – the feast day of St Dorothy. In her bedchamber at Haddon Hall, Dorothy Vernon stood alone by the tapestry, looking closely at her latest piece of embroidery.

Delicate flower patterns in gold and silver thread adorned the white satin cushion-cover which she would present later in the day to her step-grandmother, Lady Port. She smiled, well pleased with the intricate stitches of red, green and gold in the centre – a basket of flowers, the symbol of her saint, and she hoped that the lady would also be pleased with her gift, for they shared the same saint's day.

Not that this gift comes from the warmth of an affectionate heart, she reflected sadly, but from a sense of duty. She trod warily nowadays, for she did not wish to give her father or stepmother any cause for complaint against her.

Her life had been so different once, when she did not have to worry or care about being guarded in her behaviour, but basked in the love and affection to which her whole being responded. Dorothy sighed, as she looked through the window at the bleak, wintry landscape of Haddon woods. Before long the first snowdrops would appear, recalling some of her fondest memories, for once her mother had presented her with a basket of these little flowers every year as soon as they bloomed. It was a touching way of remembering her own special saint.

But then, with the coming of spring, Lady Margaret herself had faded out of this life like a fragile snowdrop. And even now, three years after her death, the thought of the first snowdrops still brought tears to Dorothy's eyes.

She was surprised, however, how much she had become resigned to her father's second marriage with the passage of time. Admittedly her relationship with her stepmother had improved a little since that day in the previous winter when, approaching the long gallery for her afternoon walk, she had overheard the echo of Sir George's voice berating Lady Maud with the words, "Dorothy is drawn by affection, not by ill looks and sour words."

Since then, polite formality had existed between them as they went about their domestic duties together. On the surface at least, she appeared to get on well with both Sir George and the new Lady of Haddon.

Still holding her embroidery, Dorothy walked across the room and sat close to the fire, where the golden threads glowed by the light of the flames. She was suddenly reminded of the treasured golden rosary given to her by Margaret and later entwined with locks of their mother's hair. Sir George had recently taken to wearing this concealed around his neck, "close to my heart," as he had said in a tone of unexpected sentimentality.

Her fears about him forcing her into an unwanted marriage had so far been dispelled – except during the anxious period last May, when it looked as though cousin Henry's return from the Scottish war would herald a betrothal between herself and his twelve year old Sudbury heir, John Vernon. Sir George had been tempted for a while by the idea of keeping Haddon in the Vernon name through this marriage. But in the end he had delayed making any firm plans for her future and seemed content that she should remain with him for as long as possible.

And then her other cousin John had come into her life! A mood of dreamy contentment came over Dorothy as she thought of him once more. Her conscience had told her that she should turn her mind away from her beloved and so, throughout the winter she had attended with great enthusiasm to her reading, needlework and music. But all to no avail! The more she tried to shut John from her mind, the more he filled her thoughts. Happy thoughts, which had brought new meaning and a great sense of belonging back into her life.

It was thus that Alice Shepney found her a few minutes later. Gently, she took the embroidery from her and placed something much smaller in her hands, her face beaming at Dorothy's cry of sheer delight.

"Another letter from Master Manners," winked the nurse. "'Tis our secret for the moment."

Dorothy broke the crimson seal and murmured softly as she read:

> *Sweetheart,*
>
> *I commend me unto you and have been as good as my word to send you greeting for your saint's day. God willing, I will see you again in the springtime and we will be happy, and talk further of the future. And if you be as I am, then say so and we shall live the better.*
>
> *So, keeping your handkerchief near my heart, till I see you I rest,*
>
> > *Yours during life in true love,*
> > *John Manners*

"In true love," she repeated out loud and kissed the letter lovingly before she regretfully consigned it to the flames. "His words will always remain in my heart, Alice, and one day I shall keep John's letters openly. They come like a breath of warm spring air to me, isolated as I am here in the winter."

"Right glad I am that my Lord of Shrewsbury's man still comes with messages for Sir George – and secret missives for you, mistress, despite the snow!" said Alice.

Dorothy went over and hugged her. "You were ever a true friend to me, Alice, and your devotion touches me deeply."

"I will always hold your happiness dear to me, even though I am little more than a pensioner now in this household."

"I will send a reply," said Dorothy, moving towards the table. "But what to say? He talks constantly of love, and though I care for him so much, what do I know of love?" She looked wistfully at the nurse. "In truth, sometimes I am afraid ..."

"Why so, mistress? You have a warm and generous heart."

"But there are doubts lurking in my mind, something Lady Gertrude, the Countess, once said to me about John's uncle and my father disagreeing. Besides, I have no wish to wed just yet or leave Haddon."

"Remember your sister," came the reply. "She was betrothed at your age, but didn't marry until she was eighteen. After three years she was eager for the match – as you will be! I believe your father will be well content to see you also wedded to the second son of an earl."

Dorothy sighed as she took up her pen. "Let's hope so. In the meantime, I shall fear no more – until the spring ..."

An April shower washed against the myriad window panes of the Haddon parlour when Sir George summoned his wife to see him.

"So the great religious upheaval begins," he blazed at her. "You must be proud of your stubborn relatives for their non-attendance at church, my lady. Three uncles imprisoned in London, another fled abroad and outlawed, and your own mother heavily fined!"

"I did try to warn her, sir," replied Maud meekly. "I have

pleaded with her repeatedly, but you know she would not listen."

"In our hearts we may continue to believe what we wish," he said. "All the law requires is that we conform outwardly to this new Church of England. But no! Some Catholics cannot even manage that. And this persecution is only the beginning!"

Lady Maud flinched, her anger rising.

"You cannot blame me for the behaviour of my relatives," she blurted out.

"No, but we owe them a certain loyalty," he retorted, "and that puts me in a very embarrassing position in this county, especially now that the new faith divides us from the Talbots. Don't you see how I am torn? Torn between conflicting loyalties!"

"It will not always be so," she tried to soothe him. "Only one life separates the throne of England from another Catholic Queen. And if Elizabeth were to die, the Queen of Scots would succeed. Surely her claim will be even stronger if the rumours are correct that she plans to return from France to Scotland."

"And who are you to instruct your husband about the English throne?" asked Sir George, his face hardening into a cold and piercing stare. "It would be better, madam, if you were at last to assume a woman's role and give me a healthy child, *preferably a son!*"

"Do you think I don't pray for that – every single day?"

"Then you should pray harder."

"Sir, I beg of you, if you have any love for me ..."

"Love?" he growled. "I did not marry you for love, my lady, but to provide me with an heir."

He left her in tears when he stalked angrily from the room, slamming the heavy oak door behind him. He felt an overwhelming urge to escape from all his troubles into the open air.

As he traversed the banqueting hall, the savoury smell of manchet bread floated along the passage from the kitchen and his careworn expression was alleviated by the sight of Dorothy treading lightly across the stone-flagged floor.

"Dorothy!" he called, stretching out his hand towards her.

She came over, eyeing him cautiously. Sir George placed his hand under her chin and jerked her face up to him.

"You have grown into a beauty, my daughter," he said proudly. "Your hair?" He appraised the auburn tresses which had been pinned up into loose folds.

"Do you approve?" she said at last. "Nurse Alice thinks it makes me look older."

She flushed with pleasure as he slowly nodded his head.

"We must get you well betrothed," he said, his face beginning to cloud again. "But that problem can wait. For the moment, go, Doll, and change into your riding habit, and then we shall ride out together, for never has the lure of the hunt attracted me so much!"

Mounted on his black horse, with the air rushing past him and his retainers close behind him, Sir George rapidly regained his good humour.

His passion for the hunt lay in the excitement of the chase and the familiar sounds from Haddon woods soon echoed along the valley – the baying of hounds, the galloping of horses, the blasting of horns and the hallooing and huing of the huntsmen themselves.

A stag had been sighted, and Sir George gave a full-blooded roar of triumph as the hunters spurred through the woodland into the open pastures, fanning out as they thundered down the slope towards the river Wye.

Despite its speed, the deer was forced to take to the water and raised its stately, antlered head as it tried to swim across.

Intent upon their quarry, no-one noticed Dorothy rein in her chestnut horse while she searched hopefully the faces of four riders who were approaching along the rutted trackway from Bakewell. The first she recognized as William Crossland, the Earl of Shrewsbury's trusted messenger, two of the others she had seen before on visits to Wingfield Manor with their master ...

And the fourth rider! She gave a sudden bounce of joy, which her horse immediately resented. He stumbled, recovered and then stood rigid, refusing to move.

John Manners rode alone towards her, his dark brown hair

reaching almost to his broad, muscular shoulders. Dorothy flapped the reins in a vain attempt to induce her horse in his direction. But there was no need, for John soon covered the distance between them.

Bright-eyed with delight, she could not think and though she tried to speak, the words would not come to her. The look of longing on her beloved's face conveyed more meaning than any words could give.

John glanced briefly down the slope, where the stag now lay dead on the other side of the river, pierced by the many arrows of its pursuers.

"You must go down to them quickly, Mistress Dorothy," he said. "Use your whip! And I will see you soon. The nurse will tell you. I come here on the Earl's business. We should be glad that he and your father are so involved in Derbyshire lead mining!"

She smiled tenderly at him and in precise tones which seemed to amuse him, she rallied herself to say, "My Lady Maud is at Haddon to receive you."

Then she gave her indignant steed a powerful swat on the rump and galloped off towards her father, while John motioned to his servants to rejoin him. Sir George, in high spirits, appeared not to have noticed her absence. Ignoring his gaping retainers, he met her full of zeal, even leaning from his saddle to embrace her with affection.

The time is right, thought Dorothy, *now*, while my father is so pleased with me. And if John asks for me, he will grant our wish, for it is a love-match. Only, I hope for a long betrothal period, like Margaret's, for I cannot commit myself totally to him just yet. In a year or two perhaps ...

She expressed only the first part of these thoughts to John after Alice had ushered her unobtrusively down to the bridge before supper. She had dressed for him specially, in her favourite gown of turqoise blue velvet, and in her happiness at finding him already waiting for her, she chattered now half-incoherently.

"There will be much business to discuss," he said, taking hold of her hands, "but in a day or two I will seek a suitable opportunity to speak with your father."

The nurse moved a discreet distance away, then John caught

Dorothy in his arms and kissed her slowly, ardently on the mouth. She clung to him as fire shot through her, and in that moment she felt the hardness of his body beneath the velvet doublet. It seemed as though her heart was merging into his, melting away her strength. He tightened his arms around her and held her fast.

"My dearest love," he whispered. "How I long for the time when we shall be together always."

"When will that be, John?" she asked, nestling contentedly against him.

"As soon as possible," he replied.

Two days later, Dorothy sat with her stepmother in the oriel window recess of the great chamber. She was trying hard to conceal her great agitation by keeping her fingers busy with a piece of embroidery, a nightcap for her father on his approaching feast day of St George.

But her mind was not on her work. Her head ached and the colours danced before her eyes, for in the parlour beneath them she knew that the whole question of her future life was being considered.

Sir George had so far treated John with all the courtesy due to an important guest, but now, having heard the young man's request, gazed relentlessly past him at the richly carved panels above the fireplace.

"My daughter, Master Manners?" he said without inflexion. "I shall have other plans for her marriage."

"But it is a love-match, sir."

The anguish on John's face still made no impression on the King of the Peak.

"It can never be," he declared. "As Dorothy's father, *I* know what is best for her."

Sir George cleared his throat with excessive thoroughness and stood up, deigning at last to look at John.

"I will speak plain with you, sir," he continued. "My daughter's dowry will be substantial, especially if I die without a male heir. And what have you to pit against that? Your lands hardly maintain you alone and even your country seats do not belong to you."

"Uffington and Wiverton are mine on long-term leases, sir," returned John without hesitation. "I sold my other estates because they were too remote, whereas Wiverton Hall is close to my brother's castle at Belvoir."

"Ah yes. Lord Rutland," mused Sir George. "No prospect of your obtaining the earldom, of course, since your noble brother already has a son to succeed him. Alas, life is hard on you younger sons of new-made earls."

He took care to stress the word 'new-made', knowing that John's father had been created the 1st Earl of Rutland, and then added more disapprovingly, "Your family has consistently supported the Protestant cause, I believe. We, the Vernons, have never done so, and this will be reflected in any alliance I choose for my daughter."

John glared at him in bitter disappointment, his handsome face etched with anger, for, in accordance with the peacock crest of his distinguished family, the young man had his pride. And Sir George had injured that pride, despite Gertrude's unheeded warning. Yet here, on the Vernon's property, John felt frustratingly powerless at this moment. The knight's implacable expression told him bluntly that the interview was over and, since the Earl of Shrewsbury's business was also concluded, he could leave Haddon whenever he wished.

Dorothy was horrified when her father informed her of his decision. Another beloved life lost to her – and this, the hardest of all to bear! A feeling of icy cold began to grip her as she tried futilely to plead with him. Sir George turned his back on her and eventually, with characteristic fury, ordered her from the parlour. And out she went, a desolate and heartbroken girl whose already shaken world had yet again keeled over ... into a frightening, formless void.

All the colour had drained from her face and she was trembling violently when she met John afterwards as promised down on the bridge. He made no attempt to hold her.

"My father laughed at me when I told him of our love for each other," she said in a low voice. "He has forbidden me ever to mention your name again."

"You were wrong about the timing," said John, his eyes downcast.

"Forgive me. I am sorry. I had no idea that he remains so loyal to our strict Papist relatives."

"He will never willingly accept for a son-in-law one who follows Her Majesty's faith. Yet I shall always love you, Dorothy. And if you love me truly, you must come away with me, in secret."

Fresh dismay swept over her, as she became conscious of the terrible new conflict now rending her.

"What, leave my father without his consent?" she sobbed. "Oh no, I cannot even think of it or bring disgrace on my family." But her voice was broken with uncertainty.

"I do not ask you to mate with a churl!" he answered defiantly.

Her face lifted valiantly to his. "I know full well of your high birth, Master Manners. But still I may not accept."

"Then I go," he said sadly. "But if ever I find a way to win you, neither walls nor waters shall separate us."

Dorothy said nothing, but merely grasped the wall of the bridge in desperation as she struggled to retain control of herself.

Before she realized, he had turned away from her and raced swiftly towards the Nether Gate, where his servants awaited him with horses.

"John!" cried a voice into the empty, gathering gloom. It was as though calling his name had taken her last drop of energy. Blinded by tears, Dorothy almost collapsed against the stone wall and buried her face in her hands.

After a while, large drops of rain began falling from the leaden sky and looking up suddenly, she was startled by a rapid movement on the water. A small black and white-breasted bird hopped onto a stone in the middle of the river, dipping up and down while it perched there.

"Only a dipper," she sighed, her hand on her heart.

And feeling a sense of kinship with the little creature, she watched it disappear completely under the water. In an instant, however, it was out again, landing on another jagged stone nearby.

As Dorothy saw the process repeated, a little hope crept into her heart. The rain splashed down on her own forlorn reflection, partially blurring its outline. Her right arm strained down from the top of the bridge to this view of herself submerged. A left arm strained up from the shape trapped in the water and when Dorothy moved round onto the bank and touched her fingers on the rippling surface, the mirrored hand readily met hers. She let it lie there for a moment, and then dipped her hand in the water before making the sign of the cross as if she had just taken holy water from the stoup at the chapel entrance.

"One day, Lord," she whispered, "one day, I would like to rise high above the water."

Then she gave a half-smile and a nod to her reflection and the girl in the water added to these a final wave before Dorothy turned back to the house.

FIVE

"Manners! That nobody!" raged Sir George. "Who gave you permission to meet him alone?"

There was no response from the girl who stood limp before him, no answering blaze on the pallid, tear-stained face which seemed to stare straight through him from beneath the tangled mass of dripping wet hair.

So, she and John had been seen making their own separate ways from the bridge. And now she would be punished. She did not care, since her life no longer held any meaning for her. Let him beat her severely; she would never tell him anything of that now-forbidden love.

"There will be no more visits to the bridge," barked her father, banging his fist on the table. "You are confined to your room and may not leave there until you are told. Now get out of my sight before I do you some harm I may later regret."

And he pushed her so violently that she was hurtled,

shrieking, into the carved oak door. Her eyes directed defiance at him as he picked herself up from the floor and then trudged wearily out of the parlour, her movements impeded by the wet clothes which clung stubbornly to her slender form.

Along the gallery leading to her chamber, she stumbled almost blindly into the arms of Alice Stepney. The nurse clucked and fussed audibly about clean towels and a dry robe, appearing to scold her for getting so wet. But once at the entrance to Dorothy's room, she pressed her hand gently, reassuringly, and a grateful look of understanding flickered across the girl's face.

No-one suspects Alice for her part in all this, thought Dorothy. Nor ever shall! She gritted her teeth in a new surge of determination.

The time passed slowly and painfully by during her period of close restraint. She did not weep, or even brood about the causes of her depression. Instead, a wild, strange restlessness seemed to possess her as every day she paced swiftly about the room, up and down, to and fro, and round the very edges of the oriel window recess. At first she tried to divert herself, by reading, working at her tapestry, or merely sitting near her window. But even at night she felt compelled to keep walking, often delving into her clothes chests or behind the richly patterned bed-curtains, as if she was searching for something, but could never find what she sought.

Dorothy saw little of her father. Still regarding her with reproach, he accepted his saint's day gift distantly from her on April 23rd. Then he returned her to the strict custody of Lady Maud, who had been assigned to this task, whether willing or not.

The guarded behaviour came back strongly to Dorothy in the presence of her stepmother, giving no hint of the turmoil which reigned within her. Always ready to respond to warmth, she could be lifted temporarily to the skies, only to be cast down to the depths again by a harsh or unpleasant word.

And so, whenever she was alone, the restlessness was let out, being added to on St Mark's Eve by the continuous chanting of a rhyme:

I sow hempseed, hempseed I sow,
He that loves me best
Come after me and mow.

"Ssh! I pray your lord father does not hear you," warned Alice, dashing into the room. She took her mistress firmly by the hand and placed her on the settle before seating herself opposite. "Besides, tis not St *Valentine*'s Eve, ladybird."

Dorothy narrowed her eyes. "I care not," she cried. "St Valentine's Eve or any eve, no servant of Sir George Vernon's will be found singing that at midnight. A pagan custom he calls it!"

She slumped down in the settle. "I wish I were free, Alice, as free as any Derbyshire village girl on that night. I cannot bear this life much longer."

She suddenly imagined herself dressed in the simple garb of a peasant girl, and, like many others, running eagerly around the outside of Bakewell Church at midnight sowing hempseed in the hope of meeting their future husbands. And when she had gone all the way round, there was John Manners waiting for her with open arms. She was seized by a deep and hopeless longing to see him again.

A longing which stayed with her and intensified as time went on. And when Sir George, after several days, allowed her to move about at liberty once more, though only around the house and gardens, still the pacing continued: up the steps to the long gallery, completing its length there and back, then briefly into the great chamber, down one staircase and up another, moving rapidly along the passages, down again, past the parlour, and so out into the gardens where the spring air was heavily scented with rosemary. Rosemary, the symbol of remembrance! From the topmost garden terrace she had a clear view of the Peveril Tower and her gaze wandered constantly there, as though in hope of seeing John return to Haddon. For Dorothy had lost him and was unable to find him, but always she must keep looking.

Very soon she had adopted that high, shady terrace as her special refuge in place of the little footbridge.

In June, the restrictions were removed altogether, on the arrival of her Vernon cousins from Sudbury. Dorothy was glad of company – any cheerful company, and the quiet good humour of young John Vernon, who was three years her junior, proved most agreeable to her. Together they spent much time playing bowls and the backgammon game of 'tables'.

"I'm glad we're friends at last," he grinned. "A year ago, you were my greatest threat!"

"And you mine," smiled Dorothy, "when they talked of our possible betrothal."

"Well, if your father refused the son of an earl for you, he would hardly consider me now – the son of a mere country squire!"

"He still bides his time," she sighed, "obviously seeking higher for me."

"The son of a Catholic earl?"

"I would rather not think of it."

"Cheer up," he said. "One day, we may share Vernon lands between us. I will be Lord of Sudbury and you the Lady of Haddon."

The idea immediately pleased her, and in childlike amusement, they addressed each other by these eminent titles, content in their new-found friendship whatever the future may bring.

On Midsummer Day, the feast of St John, the morning dawned fine and sunny, and for the first time in two months Dorothy left the confines of Haddon when she rode out with Sir George and her cousins.

The freshened air seemed to intoxicate her, whipping all the colour back into her cheeks and the liveliness into her spirit. On this, her beloved's saint's day, she would celebrate with him in thought!

Her heel spurred the white palfrey impulsively to overtake her father and outride the rest of the party.

Under a frame of low branches, over a fallen tree-trunk, scattering a herd of startled deer, Dorothy rode at full tilt, leaning forward in the saddle to goad the little mare on. Her hair cascaded from its loose folds and shone like a flame around her head when she reached the open pastures. How she relished this unbounded movement, this chance of escape ... Escape!

She gave the horse full rein, causing her to tear headlong down the hill, with Dorothy still forward on her neck.

"Doll!" came an angry shout from behind, amid the drum of horses' hooves.

She rejoindered with a quick look round, and a clear and challenging laugh.

"Come, stop me if you can!" she cried.

Cursing with fluent intensity, Sir George dug in his spurs and allowed his own horse full rein. Had the girl or her mare gone mad?

She was now nearing the foot of the hill, but the horse was beginning to tire. Sir George gained on her and saw the whip-hand raised, then an abrupt swerve, a flash of white and dark green, and Dorothy was flung sideways to land heavily, awkwardly on the ground.

He saw no more until he knelt beside her in the grass. Her eyes were closed, her face still a little flushed and warm.

"Doll, child!" he cried in a thick, hoarse voice. He slid an arm beneath her and looking up, yelled frantically for help from his pursuing companions. Her eyes fluttered open when he turned to her again and she was aware of an aching head, a fierce, gnawing pain in her leg and an anxious, familiar face bent over her. Then the sky and the ground whirled together once more into blackness.

She awoke in her bed to more pain, and to poulticing and blood-letting – and the kindly voice of her father trying to soothe her in the long-forgotten tones of her childhood.

And so father and daughter seemed reconciled. Whatever caused Mistress Dorothy's madcap flight, the story soon spread in the area around Haddon that her horse had bolted and only her great equestrian skill had saved her from more injury than a badly sprained ankle and severe bruising.

Throughout that summer, however, and well into the autumn of 1561, Dorothy's health gave cause for concern. Even the profusion of sweetly-scented roses in the gardens did not bring her their usual delight. Her face remained drawn and chalk-white, and though the stiffness and soreness had long since healed, she suffered from recurrent headaches.

"We will effect a cure at Buxton if this goes on," considered Sir George.

"She is young and time will be her balm," observed Maud. "Perhaps my lady mother is the one who should seek a cure at Buxton."

Sir George made no comment, but like his wife gazed through the parlour window towards the chapel entrance opposite. The persecution of local Catholic recusants had continued unabated, with Lady Port amongst those frequently and heavily fined. Nor could her influential friend at Court help her, for the former Bess Cavendish, now Lady St Loe, was herself a prisoner in the Tower of London for aiding the Queen's cousin in a secret marriage. Dorothy's heart had gone out to the hapless young couple concerned: to suffer imprisonment solely for the 'crime' of loving each other – how cruel and unfair the world was!

Nowadays Alice slept in her mistress's chamber, in an attempt to make her rest throughout the night. But the phase of sleep-walking had given way to nightmares by early November, and one night Dorothy awoke screaming piteously for John Manners.

The nurse came to her immediately, mopping the wet brow where damp tendrils of hair had strayed.

"Are you feverish, my child?"

"No," sobbed Dorothy convulsively. "No, Alice, it is my heart that's heavy. Tis just a year now since John told me of his love for me, and yet no word has passed between us for all these months. I think now I will never see him again."

"Not so," Alice said, sitting down by the bed. "There is a message for you, though not written, for that would be too risky at this time."

"Oh, tell me quickly," implored Dorothy.

"Master Manners asks only that you remember him, for he has neither forgotten you nor the promise he made to you."

"God bless him – and you for telling me this, Alice. When did he send the message?"

"Only a week ago," replied Alice. "I feared to tell you, mistress, for you have been so ill and I worried lest it made you worse. But now that you have spoken his name for the first time for so long ..."

"You were right to tell me," Dorothy reassured her. "How could I ever forget John?"

Smiling, the nurse stood over her once more and smoothed the girl's disordered hair. "He sent word as usual through William Crossland," she crooned, "although I'm afraid that the new Earl's man comes to Haddon rarely these days. However, Master John says that *he* will visit you again when you least expect him!"

"John ... will visit me again," murmured Dorothy, curling up in content. Now her sleep would be sound at last, for of all the news which had filtered through to her during these past months, this was easily the most welcome.

"A friend to see you!"

For a moment the words made Dorothy's cheeks glow and her heart beat with a wild hope. But as her eyes darted eagerly along the lime tree-shaded path, she saw the tall, manly figure of Thomas Stanley approach with the forbidding form of her father.

The shroud of winter had passed slowly into another spring, but so far time had worked no healing on the aching hurt of her memory.

She stood up, smoothing out the folds of her gown as she looked hesitantly from one man to the other. Thomas, handsome as ever with his curling dark brown hair and neatly trimmed beard, made the grey-bearded Sir George look even older to her than usual.

Without ceremony, Thomas advanced quickly towards her and hugged her before kissing her affectionately on both cheeks.

He then stood aghast at the sight of her, so pale, wan and fragile. Where now was that glowing beauty, that warm sparkle in her eyes and the cheerfulness of spirit which had always fascinated him?

"Where is Margaret?" she asked, making an effort to smile.

"Margaret has remained on the island," he said gently. "As you know, she is with child again, and we desperately want the child to survive this time. I have therefore come here, Dorothy, to escort you to Castle Rushen where your sister is in sore need of you."

Sir George nodded in approval.

"I shall give her whatever help and comfort I can," said Dorothy, her eyes brightening a little.

She became absorbed during the following days in the flurry of preparations for her journey. But Thomas was disturbed. He had not associated such a quality of stillness with Dorothy before. She seemed so serious, so retiring. And yet this was not like the calm serenity of Margaret. He noted her trembling hands, heard the wistfulness in her voice and soon recognized, as had no others except Alice and Countess Gertrude, the bitter loneliness in Dorothy Vernon which now obscured her lovely sheen.

He felt glad that his own sympathetic presence seemed to soften her, making her features once more beam with life and a faint rose colour deepen her cheeks.

The roadsides bloomed yellow with primroses when they set off from Haddon in early May. Attended by a maid of her own age, Dorothy bade a dutiful farewell to Sir George and Lady Maud, hoping she did not sound too happy. However hard she tried to appear doleful at parting from them, it was impossible to feel so in reality when a different world beckoned so excitingly to her – the world of the Isle of Man, where she was travelling with the Lieutenant Governor himself, her own dear brother-in-law.

What a change took place in her now that she felt free – free of sorrow, despair and resentment, and free to enjoy Thomas's company as much as ever before. She delighted in his warmth and generosity, in his kindness and infectious love of life.

"How strange that our moods can vary so much," he grinned at her, "how they change direction like the wind."

"We are at the mercy of the winds of feeling," she agreed. Yet she thought how steadfast his charm and gaiety had always seemed to her.

They were at the mercy of real winds once they reached Liverpool. Over a week went by before the weather allowed them to set sail, but delayed as they were in the Earl of Derby's castle, the mutual sympathy between them grew daily stronger. Dorothy realised fully his grief at the death of his first-born child and trusted him enough to confide her own suffering through her love and loss of John.

"We cannot always marry where the heart is, Doll," he sighed. "Such are the troubled times we live in that your father was swayed by the tribulations of my lady's kin."

"Some of them at last attended church," she told him. "But how they were heartened by Queen Mary's return to Scotland! Did you know that they loudly read forbidden Catholic books during the services? I'm afraid that didn't help their cause."

Thomas caught and held her gaze. "I for one would welcome the Queen of Scots on the English throne," he said. "The old faith survives well here in Lancashire thanks to the efforts of my father, Lord Derby. Yet even here, Elizabeth will soon impose fines and imprisonment on us."

"On us? Are you also a Papist recusant, Thomas?" asked Dorothy, disconcerted.

"No, but I incline that way."

"And Margaret?"

"She will follow where I lead. So will the Manxmen. I carry out my father's wishes on the island and Catholicism remains even stronger there."

Religion again! Oh no, not *you* of all people, she thought despondently. She half-turned away, then decided to change the subject.

"What will you call the child?"

He smiled with great boyishness as he took her hand. "If we have a daughter, what better name than Dorothy?" he said.

"Or another son?" she enthused, her face lighting up again.

"Then we shall call him Edward after my noble father."

Edward, a fine name! It suddenly made her remember

Edward Talbot, the new baby son of Countess Gertrude. She wanted to speak of him, but the words were never formed. Somehow she thought better of mentioning the Shrewsburys to Thomas.

Dorothy's natural optimism returned the next evening as they approached the Isle of Man. She had an impression of green hills and many rocks, of a strong salt tang in the air and the whirling sweep of seagulls as they darted down on the waves. The little vessel docked safely in Castletown harbour on the island's southern coast.

Castle Rushen itself had a homely, welcoming look, its high central keep adorned with a flag of scarlet and white. Protected by the river Silverburn, it was the Governor's administrative headquarters, and Thomas was received on the quayside with all due respect and ceremony.

From the minute when Margaret herself greeted Dorothy in the great hall, the girl managed to immerse herself in her love and affection for her sister. Margaret, thickened by pregnancy, no longer appeared so tall and graceful, but she was no less beautiful than before and Dorothy still admired her openly. This time her sister's prayers must be answered. She would pray with her and by her mere presence lessen the anxiety of awaiting the new baby. It would be a boy and most of all, this one would live a long life, as the other baby had not.

The whole castle pulsated with spring. Both sisters seemed awakened by it and as the sun strengthened into summer, spent as much time as they could outdoors. On an afternoon free from governmental duties, Thomas was content to watch them strolling dreamily hand in hand along the curtain wall-walk. Gentle, loving creatures both! he mused. They bloomed at present like the flowers, but what different flowers they were.

They stopped, as Dorothy pointed out some movement on the river, her face and gestures full of lively animation, while Margaret gazed happily over the parapets in gentle contemplation. As always he reminded him of a lily – calm, gracious and self-controlled. But Dorothy was as passionate and varied as a rose, sometimes golden glowing, sometimes red as fire and sometimes white as snow, when all vitality drained from her, shedding her petals to the ground.

Margaret became even more contented as her pregnancy advanced. It was on a warm August morning that she suddenly arose early and found that she must keep fully occupied. She brushed aside all help from her attendants and dressed quickly before descending purposefully to the hall.

Dorothy sauntered in there later to witness her sister violently polishing the long oak table, and judged by the tell-tale smell from the other furniture that Margaret had already been busy for some considerable time.

"What ails you?" asked Dorothy, who had grown accustomed to Margaret's recent lack of mobility.

"Nothing," she smiled, hardly looking up. "I feel so well, Doll. Such energy is a sure sign – the babe will soon be born! Don't worry, I have already sent word to Thomas and the lying-in chamber is prepared."

Dorothy marvelled that Margaret could be so calm in view of the ordeal facing her. This restlessness, this sudden activity seemed remarkable to the younger sister, yet she knew that even in this mood, Margaret still sailed on a placid sea compared with the wild tempest which had afflicted her own swift pacing during those weeks of close restraint at Haddon.

That evening, Thomas Stanley returned from his other castle at Peel on the island's west coast, to find that his wife had given birth to a son.

How soon this summer has passed, thought Dorothy. This summer of re-awakened happiness, both for herself because her memories of John no longer seemed so wounding, and for Thomas and Margaret in the form of the lively little bundle she now held in her arms.

Edward they had just christened him. His tiny hand gripped her finger with all his baby might. Yes, *this* child was thriving and Margaret was recovering satisfactorily from the birth. In a few weeks she would be able to ride out with her husband again and they would take Dorothy on that promised tour of the island, ending with prayers of thanksgiving in the cathedral at Peel. After the girl's years of loneliness, all this seemed too good to be true.

One day in October, however, Thomas was summoned unexpectedly to the landing-place outside Castle Rushen. A boat bearing the Earl of Derby's standard was fast approaching.

"Ned! What do *you* here, brother?" he laughed in surprise as a younger, thinner version of himself leapt ashore. "I thought you were abroad."

"Ah well, this French war does not appeal, even to a born soldier like me!" boasted Sir Edward Stanley. "Besides, there is a chance of fighting nearer home."

"What fighting?"

"Fighting that'll interest you, brother, if you can overcome that conscience of yours," he sneered. "How fares your good lady, Tom?"

"Well," stammered Thomas, "she is very well. And young Edward is a bonny babe."

"I envy you! Our lord father has sent me here with a gift of fine lands for you and your heir."

"*You* ... envy me! Since when, Ned?" Thomas jokingly retaliated. "You've never shown any inclination to settle down."

"True, true!" agreed his brother. "And never been pressurized to marry, being the fortunate youngest son. But lands and heirs, now that's a different matter. Gives a man status." He playfully slapped Thomas on the back as they entered the castle.

Dorothy had not seen Sir Edward Stanley since her sister's wedding, but now, meeting him after four years she took an immediate antipathy to him. At first sight, she marked, he certainly resembled Thomas, but the features were more severe – and those eyes, those cold, hard eyes which travelled avidly, approvingly up her slim body. They stared constantly at her with intent purpose, a look she clearly recognized as desire. She had seen such intentness in another man's eyes, but those expressive blue eyes had also been loving, concerned and protective. They did not threaten her like Edward Stanley's.

Nor did he endear himself to her at supper that evening. He ate and drank with abandon, and the more he drank, the rowdier he became. Even Thomas and Margaret seemed to assume harsher characters in his company. Dorothy could ill disguise her contempt at the determined way he stabbed his dagger into a venison pasty. Was he attacking a foe?

"Elizabeth is dying," he boomed, his eyes glinting as he ripped the pasty asunder. "The bastard and heretic is dying of smallpox!" He smacked his lips and shovelled an oversized piece into his mouth. "Here's to Mary of Scotland. She will restore England to the true Church of Rome."

"I will drink to that," said Thomas, raising his goblet.

"You should write to her, brother, use your position as Governor of this God-forsaken isle to support her claim to the English throne."

A shocked murmur escaped from Dorothy, while Thomas gaped, embarrassed, at his brother, over the rim of his cup. "Steady on, Ned. That would require some thought. Remember Elizabeth has not yet named her successor."

"Thought, thought!" raved Edward Stanley. "That's the trouble with you, Tom. Too much thought, too much conscience."

Dorothy hoped Thomas would issue a stinging rebuke to this insult. But no! For once she realized that his kind-heartedness was working against him, that there was, in fact, a weakness in his attractive armour – his undoubted loyalty to his formidable younger brother.

The girl was deeply distressed, for here, in Edward Stanley, she had encountered another strict Papist, and worse, he was the rash, unmarried son of a Catholic earl. And he was looking greedily at her! She had no-one to turn to, certainly not Thomas, nor Margaret either, for she, the loving and dutiful wife, was at one with her husband in all matters.

Dorothy told herself she must stay calm – and what was more, she *would* stay calm!

But the castle walls began to echo less and less to her quick and joyous laughter. She was modest and retiring in her behaviour, even timid, and always on her guard, as if attempting to shield herself from all possible attack.

She believed that her plan of campaign was succeeding. Her

solitary fantasies conjured up images of a battle formation, in which she was under siege. Her would-be suitor was not easily deterred, she soon discovered, however fruitless his efforts to parley with her proved to be. But as the days passed, Edward Stanley seemed somewhat piqued and increasingly unsure how to approach her.

Then, to her great dismay, he decided to accompany the party on her special tour of the island. Northwards they rode along the coast, past villages and watch-stations, to the northernmost Point of Ayre, and there Dorothy caught for the very first time a glimpse of the Scottish coast.

She did not wish to linger and hung back behind the other three with her attendant. This whole trip should have been so pleasant, but now she reproved herself for harbouring an odd fear she had experienced on sighting Scotland. Some turbulent force, she felt, had already been set in motion, and of herself, Margaret, Thomas and Edward Stanley, only she would be able to resist it.

They turned southwards towards Peel, but her fear turned southwards with her. She had no strength to pit against it. Not even here, in romantic Peel, as Margaret so often called it. Romantic Peel, with its castle and cathedral set together like jewels on a small and rocky islet overlooking the town.

Instead, she remembered that this place was also a prison and a terrifying creature called the Manthe Doog was said to haunt the guardroom. Several members of the island's House of Keys were waiting to see Thomas. More of a parliament than a prison, she knew, but somehow Dorothy associated its name with the latter and trembled as she thought of dark dungeons and the jangling of many keys locking in closely-confined prisoners.

But on the next day, her troubled mind found release. However briefly, however fleetingly, the peace of St Germain's Cathedral folded round her like a great pair of wings and she felt refreshed by the prayers for Margaret's son. It was with a happy lightness of heart that she returned to the open air and enjoyed a bracing walk with her sister along the battlements encompassing the islet.

"My golden rosary!" she exclaimed after a while. "And my bible too. I must have left them in the cathedral."

"Send your maid to look for them," suggested Margaret.

"Oh no, no, I must go myself. Please come with me, Margaret."

"Nay, Doll, I have orders to give for the meal now and dare not delay."

"Well, then, I will see you soon," panted Dorothy, running back with great urgency towards the cathedral. She entered a dark and empty building, but retrieved the precious items safely from under her seat. Relieved, she gabbled a quick prayer of thanks and scurried back towards the porch. She was brought to a sudden, unexpected halt and in her alarm dropped her rosary and bible to the floor. For Dorothy's way back into the outside world was now effectively blocked – by Sir Edward Stanley himself.

"We meet at last," he said vehemently, grabbing her round the waist.

Despite her confusion, she sought to hold him off.

"You wouldn't dare to insult me thus!" she heard her indignant voice protesting. "My father will wreak a bitter vengeance on you."

"So there is spirit in you after all!" His laughter mocked her. "I am prepared to risk the friendship between our two fathers."

He pressed her so cruelly tight against him that she fought for breath and then began fighting him, kicking out at him furiously. His hold on her loosened enough for her to scream, as she lashed out at him in terror, beating him with her fists and clawing with her nails until one of her blows drew blood from his left cheek. Without thinking, he raised one hand to his face.

"Little spit-cat!" he cursed her.

She tried to wrench herself free, but his other arm gripped her more tightly. She screamed out again, so that she barely heard the sound of footsteps running towards them. A pair of hands suddenly clamped on Edward Stanley's shoulders and jerked him away from Dorothy, who fell to her knees, sobbing.

"God's death, brother," said Thomas. "Must you indulge your lust *here*?"

He leaned down and coaxed the frightened girl to her feet. He then picked up her bible and rosary and placed them in her shaking hand. "Thomas," she whimpered, "th-thank you."

"I find your conduct disgusting," he glowered at his brother. "You have wilfully insulted this lady, who is at present in my charge."

"I have not!" shouted Edward Stanley. "She's bewitched me."

"The spell is your own lust, you mean!"

"Nay, Tom," he wheedled, gazing unperturbed at Dorothy. "I wish to marry her."

"Oh no," said Dorothy, shrinking closer to her rescuer. "I couldn't."

"Come with me to Margaret now," Thomas tried to soothe her. "As for you, Ned, this hasty offer of marriage does not condone your behaviour. However, Dorothy would be a good match for you – in more ways than one! I will talk to you later."

But as they turned to leave him, Edward Stanley had one parting shot.

"No woman follows her own inclination in marriage," he taunted Dorothy. "Our two families share the same faith and I am sure of your father's consent. How can you, a chit of seventeen, bear up against the will of a father like yours?"

How indeed! She moved disdainfully away from him while Thomas dismissed the worried group of servants who had gathered.

Here, she considered, following her brother-in-law the short distance back to the castle, I have no true place now. No true friends either? For surely, wouldn't Thomas and Margaret agree with this latest bid for her hand?

Margaret, however, was gentle when she saw her sister's dishevelled appearance. "You're hurt, love?" she enquired. "You look as though you've seen the Manthe Doog! I'll get some wine to warm you."

"Thank you," whispered Dorothy, and then, "No, I don't need any nursing."

"What happened?"

"The fault lies with my brother," explained Thomas, and went on to relate the incident to Margaret in a voice of biting calm, while Dorothy sipped at her wine.

"It is only right and fitting," observed Margaret, "that Ned should make up for his offence by honouring Dorothy in marriage."

"But I'm sure he was only just saying that!" cried Dorothy.

"Hush! To be joined in holy wedlock to a Stanley would be an excellent match for you."

Dorothy turned piteous, pleading eyes to Thomas, but he told her truthfully, "Ned will apologize for his conduct towards you, Dorothy, that I shall ensure. But if he is determined enough to wed, I would not care to gainsay him, for marriage is indeed the most honourable solution. Your father will be pleased to make you a daughter of the house of Derby."

Margaret smiled acquiescently at him and even more heightened her sister's distress. But Dorothy, as she dragged herself tearfully away to smarten her appearance in time for the forthcoming meal, knew that her spirit had erupted to rebel totally against this proposed marriage. And soon the violence of her renewed longing for John took even her by surprise. Gradually, during those placid summer days she thought she had trained herself to dwell on him without suffering, and now she realized fully how much the coming of Thomas's brother had upset that hard-won equilibrium.

John! What a little fool I was to let him go, reflected this older Dorothy, thinking back to the previous year.

Now in her mind she lived with him and was haunted by him. By day she imagined that he walked and talked with her, at night that he called to her through the darkness, his hands reaching out, but never touched. Such nights quickly showed in her face, and both Thomas and Margaret, seeing this, wanted to comfort her but could not. They could not entirely understand her sorrow, for they did not see Edward Stanley through her eyes.

Back at Castle Rushen on the night of Hallowe'en, a storm arose. Rain spattered against the window panes of Dorothy's chamber, strong gusts of wind roared against the thick castle walls and the wild restlessness welled up in her again until it could not be withstood. Away out there was the storm, as restless as she was, and a voice was calling to her.

No-one could stop the distracted girl as she sped down the steep spiral staircase and eventually emerged onto the curtain wall-walk. She strode with confidence into the wind and driving rain, her head up, her cloak flying about her, unaware of anything except reaching the owner of that voice.

Presently she halted, looked out over the river and remembered that much smaller river at Haddon. She remembered too the special dream she had built up so long ago. Now she had no doubt that John's face and that of the young husband walking with her in the sunlight were both the same.

Now she also heard clearly someone calling her name behind her. She turned, pushing back her streaming wet hair and spied a tall figure running towards her. She stood in desperate disappointment, realizing that it was Thomas when she had hoped so much for John. Her imaginings had seemed so real.

Thomas came up to her, breathing fast.

"In God's name, Doll ... You're drenched!"

She stared down vaguely at the dark folds of her cloak and he, moved by compassion for her plight, put out his hand towards her.

She recoiled from him, her hands shielding her as if to ward off a blow.

"Don't touch me!" she shrieked. "You all handle me like I am some plaything." Then her face crumpled as she burst into tears.

"You must calm yourself," he told her.

"I didn't mean it! Please forgive me, Thomas, you are a good man."

She suddenly clutched his hand and her eyes widened as she looked out once more over the river Silverburn. "I love to watch the river wending its way to the sea," she said. "Oh, please understand, Thomas! You know I must follow that river."

"We shall arrange for your journey home," he said.

SIX

When Dorothy returned to Haddon, the considerable preparations for Christmas had already begun, and her father talked constantly of the great hunting festival he planned in the early spring. The King of the Peak still reigned!

She became caught up in the general atmosphere of festivity, despite her own melancholy and the dread she felt about her future. She had reached the depths of despair during that storm on Hallowe'en and never again would she allow herself to sink so low.

Now she lived from one day to the next and was thankful for "each day's little kindness", as she often told Alice. In her sadness. life had brought her unlooked-for compensations. Never before had she appreciated the power of prayer, but then she had never prayed with such meaningful intensity until recent months. And the two wishes she had prayed for most had been granted, for her nephew continued to thrive and Queen Elizabeth had recovered from that near-fatal illness.

Dorothy's prayers were now for her own future. As though in response, four lines of a psalm had come to her notice. They provided all she wanted to say:

> *In thee, Oh Lord, have I trusted, my hope is all in thee,*
> *Let not confusion me oppress, nor once take hold on me*
> *But rid me from all my troubles, in they great righteousness,*
> *Incline thine ear unto my words and save me from distress.*

She memorized these words, she prayed them every day. Had the tide turned at last in her favour? She hardly dared to hope. But at least some of that wild restlessness had been channelled away from her.

One morning Sir George rode off with some servants to his Staffordshire home at Harlaston. He said nothing to Dorothy, except that he would be away for several days. How like him! she thought. She knew only too well that he was going to negotiate the marriage contract between herself and Edward Stanley. She managed to quell her anger. Such a transaction would take time, and she hoped it would be a very long time before she saw Thomas's brother again.

Lady Maud was much preoccupied with Christmas preparations and so left the girl to herself. As always Dorothy was thinking of John, wondering how thing were with him, how she could get in touch with him. There was so much she did not know about him, yet in her dreams she felt she knew him completely. And she knew that he would always answer the greatest need in her – the need to feel loved and protected. No other man could be her fortress against a world which had almost crushed her and at the same time her gateway to a happy, fulfilled life.

She was still thinking of him as someone far away when the sound of raucous laughter in the courtyard drew her to the window.

She witnessed a lively scene below, as a shifting, expectant throng of local people clamoured round a pedlar for a glimpse of his treasures.

"What is't ye lack?" he kept crying. "Fine bone lace or edgings, sweet gloves, silk garters, very fine combs ... What is't ye lack?"

"Nowt but a wife!" called one of a newly-arrived band of minstrels.

"Silk or fine wrought?" retorted the pedlar.

"Nay, lad, fine boned!"

And so the exchanges went on for several minutes to occasional outbursts of laughter and applause. The minstrel spoke in a broad, flat accent which Dorothy could not place, though she assumed it to be of the north country. But as her attention focussed upon him, she simply could not believe her eyes. She told herself firmly that she could not make her lover appear merely by thinking of him. If only she could!

No, this was someone else, although admittedly someone rather like him. However, there was no mistaking the minstrel's ease of manner or his lively banter. Despite the rough accent and even rougher, travel-stained clothes, there was enough likeness of John in that tall figure to twist her heart.

The midday meal which followed seemed to drag on interminably, but Dorothy's gentle bearing did not betray her feelings. She would not permit her eyes to stray towards the minstrel's gallery and it was almost as if she had deliberately donned a mask to hide her real self – or so she thought, until a haunting melody rippled through the hall and the hooded lute player at the back began to sing. Melting sweetness flowed through her, memories of the same rich voice she had heard once before at Wingfield Manor and many times since then in her dreams. She fought hard to maintain her composure, but realized it was a losing battle.

"Might I retire now to my chamber?" she asked her stepmother. "I fear my head aches again."

Maud regarded her coldly. "You may go," she said in a dull, tight voice.

Dorothy sighed as she rose from her seat. Had anyone ever aroused a spark of sympathy in this unhappy young woman? She provided living proof of how wretched an enforced marriage could be. The girl gave a quick curtsey, then picking up her skirts she fled from the hall and almost flew up the nearby stairs. But reappearing on the side gallery of the hall, she walked slowly along with her bright gaze fixed eagerly on the minstrels' gallery. Across the huddle of musicians a pair of vivid blue eyes met hers in a fleeting look of tenderness. Dorothy and John were aware of each other for the first time since their parting.

She skipped lightly across the landing to her chamber. Here indeed was a strange situation, but how exciting it was! She knew that it could not continue as it was for long and she was amazed to find herself a little frightened now that this was reality and no longer a dream. After all this time, a small part of her still wanted to go on being pursued and loved from a distance, but uncaught.

She paced anxiously up and down her room until she heard Alice enter the old nursery next door. The old woman was moving to and fro in the rocking chair when Dorothy entered, but her greeting was cut short as the girl suddenly flung herself at her feet and began weeping into her lap.

"Why, sweet lady, what is the matter? Has Dame Maud been cross with you again?"

"No, Alice. It is *he*, it is John, returned to Haddon at last. Oh, thank God he has come!"

And babbling on, she acquainted Alice with the details of her day so far.

"Twill not be long, my pretty one, before you see Master John again," promised her dear confidante. "I think I will hie me down to the menials' quarters and try to seek him out."

"Go ... go now!" the girl exhorted her, and Alice willingly agreed.

But for Dorothy there were more tears, more swift paces, until the nurse eventually came back with a message. "Five o'clock by the third elm of the avenue, all being well," she said.

All was well for the secret meeting. Sir George was away, Lady Maud was supervising all work in the kitchens and the short December day was fading rapidly.

John stood within the shadow of the trees leading up to the bowling-green and no sooner had Dorothy joined him than he took her hand and drew her also into their shelter.

As Alice moved away to keep watch, Dorothy was aware of a more than physical sense of safety and warmth, for she had found once more the sheltering tree of her very own, whose feelings for her had endured.

"Sweetheart," he said, "I have lived a lifetime since we parted."

"And we have both suffered much," she replied with quiet conviction. "John, if only you could have come sooner."

"I came here last spring, but to my dismay you had already gone. Since then, I have lived some time in remotest Yorkshire awaiting news of your return."

"So now we have both – returned." There was a note of anticipation in her voice.

He drew her closer to him. "Dorothy, my friends believe that I am now fighting in France. Instead, I have risked coming here to see whether at last you know your own heart, or whether I should after all join my youngest brother in aiding the French Protestants."

She felt a tremor of apprehension as his arms folded tightly round her. "John ..." she began weakly.

But he interrupted her, "You cannot deny that you still love me. Dorothy, why did you say me nay?"

"I – I thought that to you I was still a foolish child."

"You know full well what you are to me."

His voice was so caressing that all tension left her. She put her arms around his neck and they kissed fervently, passionately.

"You know that I love you and cannot exist without you," he murmured, then kissed her again.

In these moments of tenderness, all the pent-up loneliness in Dorothy Vernon was finally swept away. If differing religions and conflicting affections could not be reconciled, so be it. Her commitment to him was total. She loved him, trusted him absolutely and no longer hesitated to place her future in his hands.

Looking into her flushed and eager face, John believed that she was suddenly so determined to marry him that she did not see the enormous difficulties which still lay before them.

"We must now think of a plan," he said, "and get you away from here safely, without fear of pursuit."

"Yes, but please think quickly."

"Dorothy, we must be very careful not to bring suspicion upon ourselves. It would not do for others to know what is in our minds."

"I trust your judgement, John. But do not under-estimate the courage of either of us."

"I would never do that," he teased her. "My bold little princess! Be patient a little while longer, for the winter sets in and to escape from your father's wrath, we must travel far away from here."

Impulsively she kissed him with great affection, such joy, such clear purpose she had not felt in her life for a long time.

"Where will we go?" she asked lightly.

"To my former manor, at Thornton-in-Craven."

"Your manor has a pretty name."

A look of deep seriousness came into his face. "Sweetheart, it is bleak and inaccessible at this time of year. The journey there would be too frightful for you."

"But we could ride to Wiverton instead," ventured Dorothy.

"I do not think so," he told her gently. "My country seat is too close to Haddon. For the time being I will contrive to stay around here and see you whenever I can."

They heard Alice approach.

"It would be well to go now, mistress," she said, smiling fondly from one to the other.

She turned her back on them again and for a moment they clung to each other.

"God keep you safe, John," whispered Dorothy. "I tremble at the risks you run for my sake."

"We must both take the greatest care. Only a little while, my love, and then our happiness will be complete."

He kissed her once more, then watched longingly as the girl and her companion walked back towards the house.

The winter was indeed bitterly cold, and the makeshift, rutted roads became icy and dangerous. Yet Dorothy felt a warm glow inside her, as if bleakness and isolation would never again invade her heart. She lived only to see John and all her restless energy now gathered itself into a resolute purpose. There must be no hint of suspicion, no cause for complaint against her. She took care, particularly during the Christmas celebrations, to display the greatest courtesy towards everyone. In striving for the necessary secrecy and caution, she had discovered in herself a firmness of mind and self-control she never knew she possessed.

A firmness of mind and calm judgement to equal that of her lover. A conspiracy of silence was maintained through the goodwill of Alice and a handful of carefully-chosen servants, for John had disguised himself as a forester, wild and unkempt in appearance, though still comely in his coarse leather jerkin and rough green cloak.

"There is an aura of strength about you, whatever you wear," confided Dorothy. "And I too feel strong when you are near me."

"You are so much part of me," said John. "My happiness comes from yours."

As their love for each other deepened, so did the friendship and understanding between them. So often their whispered meetings were restricted to chill wintry nights after the household had retired. Then John could steal forth unobserved from the woods, converse with his beloved through the open window of her chamber and be ready to plunge back into the shadowed safety of the trees at the first sign of danger. They were constantly on the alert, their eyes and ears open to any unwelcome intrusion.

That younger Dorothy, she thought with an air of maturity, would have followed her instincts and leapt straight into John's arms from her window, heedless that she might injure him or herself. Now she considered how the ground sloped away downhill beneath her first-floor window – and perhaps it was just a little too high to leap from!

On her saint's day, Dorothy's overwhelming delight was mingled with consternation and alarm when John unexpectedly entered her room armed with a pile of faggots.

"The fires of Haddon are hungry at this time of year," he said lightly, "as I am to see you." He removed the hood of his cloak. "Don't be afraid, sweetheart. Your faithful Alice is standing guard."

Then laughing, he swept her into his arms and kissed her smiling mouth. "It seems that living in these savage woods has so changed my appearance that Sir George Vernon does not recognize me!"

The girl was relieved, but still speechless and dazed with disbelief at his cool nerve. That he could walk about her father's house unrecognized! It was all going so simply and smoothly, this secret love, *too* simply, and as Dorothy suddenly found out in early March, far too smoothly.

She sent an urgent, agitated message to John through Alice and after several unsuccessful attempts to meet, they came together at last on the ill-frequented bowling-green, well hidden by the high encircling yew hedge.

She grasped his hands with fierce determination.

"John, what shall we do? My father has bid me receive another as my husband."

"Then we must make for the north without delay."

"But how?" she wept. "I have no idea how many eyes will be watching me from now on. I think, I dream of escape, but I cannot plan."

His arms were round her, supporting and comforting her.

"I will find a way."

Her eyes suddenly brightened. "At the hunting festival, there will be a multitude of guests ..."

They understood each other. "Then any vigil on you will have to be relaxed," he smiled. "And amid all the revels, my Dorothy, we shall flee!"

She rejoiced in his strength, his resolution cool and composed as hers was burning, passionate, but just as unwavering. He was the firm ground beneath her, the solid rock to hold her steady, for now her bold spirit mutinied, so wide was the rift she felt between herself and the rest of her family. The last thread of her dutiful loyalty had finally snapped.

"I would obey my father in all other matters," she affirmed. "But he shall not force me into this! I would rather die than become Sir Edward Stanley's wife."

"Dear heart, you shall be mine before this month is out."

Dorothy's whole body relaxed at his words and he clasped her to him in the embrace which sealed his promise. She met his lips without faltering, and when he presently released her, still she stayed close to him.

They exchanged more hurried words as Alice came near to accompany her mistress back to her room. John took Dorothy in his arms again and kissed her, gently this time. "Until the hunting festival, my love," he whispered. "Then we shall be together – and for always."

"God be with you, John."

They said their farewells, and Dorothy left him, knowing that the next part of blustery March would seem more like a year to her, deprived of his company while he finalized the plans for their flight. But at least she could live without the constant fear of discovery, of John being struck down at any minute by her father's sword, and for that she felt truly grateful.

A quiet mood came over her when she returned to her firelit chamber. So near, yet still so far away seemed the promise of the happy future which she herself had chosen. Ahead of her now was the final barrier, like a stone wall, sharp edged and blocking her clear view of the horizon. She had to reach the other side; she could not afford to fail, for if she did, her life would become intolerable. The stone wall would then enclose her, making her delicate hands bleed as they beat hopelessly against it.

So the need for secrecy and caution about her love for John was now greater than ever. And Dorothy knew that these few peaceful moments alone in her chamber were merely the calm before the approaching storm, for the hunting festival would be the severest test yet of her self-control.

She nodded and smiled as her maid, Joan Lomas, came in to light the candles. The girl responded with an equal warmth, a sustaining friend had she proved to her mistress in adversity and staunchly loyal since their return from the Isle of Man.

The candles reflected in the window panes, tiny, quivering flowers of flame against the gathering dusk. Tiny flowers like the first crocuses now pushing their way through in the Haddon gardens. Images suddenly poured through Dorothy's mind and the warm glow inside her produced a new surge of confidence. She thought of crocuses and the coming of spring, the season for lovers, with all its tender green promise of new life. And green itself, the colour of true love. So ... if she felt in any danger of losing her self-control, all she had to do was remember these crocuses of candlelight. Then she would keep calm.

The hunting festival brought together most of the leading local families and for Dorothy, meeting Edward Stanley again, the atmosphere seemed knife-edged. He made a stiff, formal bow before her, muttering some small courteous phrase of greeting. She avoided his direct gaze, that triumphant, faintly mocking expression on his face.

You are not the only one who can use courtesy as a weapon, she thought determinedly. Her aversion to him had not lessened and her instinct was to repay him with a look of fierce contempt. But no, that would be disastrous. Instead, she put on her sweetest smile and made a graceful curtsey, then, since she must not single out anyone for too particular attention, she inclined her head politely and, her composure unruffled, moved on to receive other guests.

The Earl and Countess of Shrewsbury had arrived with a large retinue of retainers, Lady Gertrude having braved the difficult roads in a litter despite yet another pregnancy. She was so desirous to see Dorothy again and her natural sympathy for the girl caused a glance of easy affection to pass between them immediately.

"I wish you every happiness, my dear," said Gertrude, embracing her.

"Thank you," replied Dorothy in the pleasant social tone she was using towards everyone. She did not really wish to thank anyone or be reminded about her father's intentions to betroth her to Edward Stanley. And the Countess's untimely reminder had checked any impulse to welcome her with the usual warmth.

However, she was glad of Gertrude's presence, if only because it diverted her away from the unwanted attentions of Edward Stanley, whom she noticed drinking very heavily and noisily with her father.

She was excused from joining the first day's hunt, Sir George being anxious to comply with Gertrude's request for her company. They spent the afternoon parading the length of the long gallery, talking mostly of Gertrude's children, especially the coming baby. And Dorothy seemed keen to listen to the details of the cradle, the clothes being prepared and arrangements for the lying-in. Anything but dwell on the subject of her own future!

Then the Countess took her arm and said quietly, "Who knows, perhaps you will be making similar preparations before too long."

Dorothy smiled and answered politely, "Ah yes, I hope to have many children."

But any further enquiries about her future were charmingly dismissed.

Gertrude watched her, frowning, a little puzzled, as Dorothy invited her to join a group of other ladies for a gentle game of 'troll-my-dames'. The girl mildly congratulated herself, for she had greatly feared that she would feel tempted to tell Gertrude the secret of her heart. And why not? After all, the lady was John's sister and her own kind friend. But then she had done nothing to help John in the matter, nor even spoken of him this day.

And Dorothy had just discovered that Gertrude was no more sentimental about marriage than anyone else. "Parents arrange their children's marriages for prosperity," she had emphasized, and that was the way she had recently married off her eldest son and daughter. Of happiness, of love, she had made no mention. So, although Gertrude had found Dorothy clothed in velvet during their time together, under the soft exterior was an impression of steel she had not connected with her before.

That night, Dorothy readily asked her father's permission to take part in the next day's hunt.

With the wind swirling all around them, they went riding to the chase. Over frost-hardened pastures, through woods and undergrowth, and out again at full gallop across wild stretches of moorland, they followed their prey to a good day's sport.

Resounding cheers filled the air as Sir George and Edward Stanley each felled a proud stag.

"The harquebuss, that foreign weapon!" grimaced Sir George, himself an excellent archer.

"The weapon of the future!" returned his boisterous companion. "What think you, Mistress Dorothy?" He put out his hand towards her.

"I?" she replied, pulling her horse skilfully away from him. "I regret, sir, as a mere woman, I know nothing of such matters." She lowered her eyes modestly, averting her gaze from his stony expression.

After that he left her well alone, though the wind did later carry to her some distant talk, amid great guffaws of male laughter of young virgins becoming warm and yielding once a man had possessed them.

She shuddered, turning over in her mind wild, impossible

plans for escape. But with much difficulty, calmness prevailed on the homeward journey and a hopeful voice inside her seemed to whisper on the wind, "John, please come soon!"

All during the next day, a rich stream of smoke and savoury smells sallied forth from the Haddon kitchens, in preparation for the great banquet to be held that evening. Minstrels arrived from all parts, including the north, and the poor also arrived in plenty, for Sir George was keeping open house as the climax to his hunting festival.

It was after the meal and the ladies had retired to the side gallery of the banqueting hall that a cry went up, accompanied by loud cheering, "A song for the Princess of the Peak! A song in praise of her beauty!"

All eyes were turned towards Dorothy and many cups were raised.

"You, the lute player," continued Edward Stanley, "I have heard your skill. A song for the fair Dorothy!"

All eyes were now turned towards the minstrels' gallery. Briefly, Dorothy met John's embarrassed gaze with a look of great sympathy. Oh no, nothing could go wrong with their plans at this late stage. Silently, she began to pray, while John waited for the din to subside. He remained seated at the back behind a harper, his face half-hidden by the hood of his cloak. He took up his lute and sang:

> *Last night a proud page came to me*
> *Sir Knight, he said, I greet you free*
> *The moon is up at midnight's hour*
> *All mute and lonely is the bower.*
> *To rouse the deer my lord is gone*
> *And his fair daughter's all alone*
> *As lily fair and as sweet to see.*
> *Arise, Sir Knight, and follow me.*
>
> *The stars streamed out, the new-woke moon*
> *O'er Chatsworth hill gleamed brightly down,*
> *And my love's cheeks, half-seen, half-hid,*
> *With love and joy blushed deeply red.*
> *Short was our time and chaste our bliss,*

A whispered vow and a gentle kiss
And one of those long looks which Earth
With all its glory is not worth.

The stars beamed lovelier from the sky,
The smiling brook flowed gentlier by.
Life, fly thou on, I'll mind that hour
Of sacred love in greenwood bower.
Let seas between us swell and sound,
Still at her name my heart shall bound.
Her name – which like a spell I'll keep,
To soothe me and to charm my sleep.

During the last verse, Dorothy's eyes wandered towards Gertrude, who was standing nearby, spellbound, with a look of bewildered recognition on her face. From there she looked towards the Earl and noticed a similar, perplexed expression as he turned to listen to her father.

And when she looked at *him*, Dorothy's heart sank. Sir George's eyes were blazing in a face like thunder. Above all the applause, he addressed the Earl with harsh candour, "Let seas between us swell and sound indeed! Let John Manners' song be prophetic for Derbyshire, for England has no river deep or wide enough to save him from a father's sword, whose peace he seeks to wound."

Shrewsbury gave him back look for look, level and unmoving. "What you say to me is gibberish. My brother-in-law fights for Her Majesty in France."

Sir George was not convinced. "My lord, if I find him here at Haddon, he shall be chained up in the deepest dungeon."

"Whatever your quarrel with him," said the Earl curtly, "I tell you this. If John sought my aid in any matter, in my friendship for him I would not refuse."

Cursing under his breath, Sir George then turned his darkened gaze on Dorothy and a feeling of dread rushed through her when he beckoned to her to leave the hall.

She met him in the great chamber, alone. Her stiffest test yet and so near to achieving her hopes! She intended to play her role well, the modest, obedient daughter intent on his every word. And fortunately for her, he softened at her gentle courtesy.

"Dorothy," he said hoarsely, "drink has done more than impaired the wits of our guests tonight. They look at you with bolder eyes and speak of you with a bolder tongue than I could wish."

She kept her eyes lowered, praying that John would slip away unhindered from the hall. "Perhaps I should retire to my chamber," she suggested quietly.

"Yes, yes," he agreed. "'Tis pity indeed that you must go there so early. But let the wise Alice be with you, and I will see you in the morning."

He kissed her forehead and she curtsied before they took their leave of each other – he to return to his guests and she to the uneasy silence of her room.

Alice and Joan were already there, watching and waiting, the nurse preparing a small bundle for her mistress's use, the maid standing rigid by the recessed window lending her ears to every sound.

In great haste, Dorothy changed from her gown of gold damask into one of grey woollen kersey and Alice wrapped a plain brown cloak around her.

There was no time for more, for at that moment came the owl signal which marked the beginning of Dorothy's journey north with John.

SEVEN

"Still at her name my heart shall bound." The words were still ringing in Gertrude's ears as she and her husband retired to their apartments. Sir George, she had noticed, had returned to his wine-cup with a vigour and mirth undimmed by his brief absence from the hall.

But Dorothy had not come back and Gertrude felt a lively concern, unwilling though she was to interfere between a father and his daughter. And yet ... that shadow of dread across the girl's face when Sir George called her away, was unforgettable. Poor Dorothy, thought Gertrude. She had seemed so much happier until that moment – older, yes, and with notably more poise –

"My dear, your eyes are wearing their brooding look," said the Earl. "Come, unburden yourself by my side."

They sat down together while she mused, "I was merely marvelling, George, how the youngest of the Vernons has grown up."

"Young Dorothy? Aye, she's a pretty lass. I'll warrant she'll lead Sir Stanley out there a merry dance."

"That she will," smiled Gertrude. "But there's something about the girl – some corner of this new Dorothy eluding me." She shrugged. "I cannot help myself, I have a maternal interest in her ..."

"Well, an enquiry after her welfare would be a courteous gesture tomorrow," suggested Shrewsbury.

Gertrude agreed, and then he went on with a knowing look, "But surely, there is something more important bothering you?"

"Yes, George. Uncanny, is it not, how a menial minstrel can sing so much like my brother?"

"If you mean Master John, yes," he replied, putting his arm around her. "But I believe my lady had a clearer view of him than I."

"No. He was muffled up in his cloak. It was his voice which caught my attention."

Shrewsbury's face clouded. "It was the song which caught Sir George Vernon's attention. He made a very pointed remark to me about your brother."

"What did he say?"

"That he would cast him into the deepest dungeon if he ever finds him here."

In the brief, shocked silence which followed, anger suddenly flashed from Gertrude's blue eyes almost like a living flame. But the Earl regarded her, deeply troubled, and her consideration for him held her in check.

"The minstrel, my dearest lord," she said, "I was so busy

watching Dorothy that I didn't see him leave the hall. Otherwise I would have sent for him ..."

"Gertrude," tut-tutted the Earl, and then asked directly, "what *is* going on in this cauldron of intrigue?"

"I wish I knew."

"You know your brother," he said softly, "perhaps better than most."

She smiled at him, warmed by his unfailing gentleness towards her and her family.

"It would seem I know very little nowadays," she replied. "John told me once of his love for Dorothy Vernon. He sought my help in gaining her father's consent, but I could not ignore the religious gulf between our family and hers. And so I advised him against the match. I could see our influence with Sir George already waning."

"You gave sound advice," her husband reassured her.

"But he persisted," continued Gertrude, "said he believed that Dorothy loved him. He aimed to find out, but I heard nothing more."

"Has Dorothy spoken of him?"

"No, and I thought wiser not to mention him, especially now that she is promised elsewhere."

Shrewsbury stared gravely into the crackling fire. "I am convinced you should see the girl," he decided. "Go to her chamber and make sure that all is well with her."

"Immediately?"

"Yes, my dear. We cannot wait until the morning."

Gertrude readily assented. Circumstances dictated this nocturnal visit. Besides, their interest was now alight, both hers and the Earl's, and he was not likely to let the matter rest there. She had seen that fixity of purpose on his dear, serious face before, every deep-gouged line telling of the sympathy which belied a surprising determination.

Shouts of drunken laughter from the hall almost drowned out her tapping on the door of Dorothy's bedchamber. The door opened very slightly and a pair of wary eyes peered out at her.

"My Lady Countess!" gasped Joan, and bobbed an awkward curtsey.

"I must speak with your mistress," said Gertrude with her usual confiding smile.

"But Mistress Dorothy is asleep, my lady," whispered the maid.

"Even so, I would reassure myself that she is well."

Gertrude raised her voice intentionally in response, which led an older, more respectful voice to answer, "Please come in, my lady."

And Alice suggested, speaking very low, that perhaps her ladyship would care to warm herself by the fire for a moment. Ushering Gertrude across the room, she tiptoed past the bed where "Mistress Dorothy, poor lamb" now slept and around which the curtains had been fully drawn. Joan silently shut the door, while Alice told the lady that Dorothy was indeed well and would sleep soundly till the morning, having been administered a hot posset by her good self. But if "my lady" wished her to give any message to Dorothy in the morning, she would gladly do so.

Gertrude rubbed her hands by the fire, saying, "No, there is no message and I will not wake her now."

The two servants thanked her agreeably and made to conduct her back to the door. "But I would rest easier in my own bed if I could just take a peep at her," she asserted with equal sweetness, manoeuvring herself to the bed.

The two servants then stood like statues while the Countess took her "peep". Sharply, she widened the gap in the bed-curtains as she exclaimed at her discovery.

"Where is your mistress?" she asked, her head placed quizzically on one side as if she sought the truth from two of her children.

"I am afraid I cannot say, madam," replied Alice distantly.

"I know of your loyalty to her," Gertrude assured them both. "I too am very fond of Mistress Dorothy. So you can trust me: if anything is amiss, I guarantee that no harm will come to either of you." Her eyes wandered from Alice to Joan. "*Is* aught amiss?"

Joan swallowed, glazing her eyes beyond Gertrude at the bed, but Alice, drawn perhaps by the lady's past kindness to Dorothy, now seemed a little more accessible.

The Countess told them to be seated and then walked to stand near the nurse. "Please tell me," she said, "does this also concern my brother, John?"

"Yes, lady," the old woman whispered.

"So now," said Gertrude more warmly, "we have come together – we who love them both so well."

She questioningly traced a heart-shape in the air and smiled when Alice nodded.

"If only you could've seen them together, my lady," snuffled Joan sentimentally.

"Lord Shrewsbury and I would help them if we could," Gertrude added.

"My lady, I fear it is too late to help them," said Alice. "The young pair have eloped without telling us their destination."

Gertrude then astounded them by emitting an uncharacteristic oath. "We shall find out their destination," she insisted, excusing herself. "You must understand that I misjudged the love between these two and I wish now with all my heart to make amends. My brother and his lady will be married, but not secretly I hope. I will not stand by to see Dorothy disinherited by her father."

She now had the look of a purposeful woman with her head up into a wind and the glow of a glittering promise on her face. "Please accompany me to the Earl, both of you," she said.

And followed by Alice and Joan, the Countess went back to her own apartments.

Shrewsbury was exultant when she told him what had happened. "Well, well, well!" he chuckled. "It pleases me to hear that John is in love at long last. But I never thought of a young country girl bearing him off!"

Then the urgency of his wife's manner made him consider the matter more solemnly again.

"Aye, there is some stern talking to be done. Believe me, my lady, we shall use whatever power and influence we have to bring about this marriage."

"If we do, then John might one day be Lord of Haddon."

"And our strong, reliable friend! Who knows, this might be the wisest move we have ever made."

Gertrude expressed her relief at his use of the word 'we' since

this meant he needed her with him. She could not let him tackle
Sir George alone, yet she had worried in case he reminded her of
her condition in his indulgent way and insisted upon her resting.

Rest, when such speedy action was now required? That was the
last wish on her mind!

When the Shrewsburys, the Vernons and Sir Edward Stanley
had assembled in the parlour, Sir George bowed before
Gertrude with his usual formality.

All due respect shown for my rank, she sighed to herself, I
cannot fault him on that.

However, as always she could sense the web of tension
between them: always unspoken and disguised by the courtesy
which custom demanded. Real feelings may be hidden beneath
the surface, but still they lived! Fate had once woven its own web
around a Manners-Vernon wedding and now the demeanour of
Dorothy's father increased Gertrude's determination even more
to negotiate a second marriage between his family and hers – and
with full parental approval. She needed only to glance at the
Earl's grim features to know she had inspired him well.

Shrewsbury broke the news of Dorothy's elopement.

"What!" cried Sir George. "My lord, you are surely jesting."

But the Earl and Countess remained coldly impassive and the
Vernon's remark had been intended only to cover his own acute
embarrassment. He was still sober enough to read the look of
warning on Shrewsbury's face: there would be no more
thundering rages.

Edward Stanley stood in the shadows behind Sir George, his
hand placed meaningfully on the hilt of his sword. Bright and
somewhat glassy-eyed until a few moments before, he had been
abruptly sobered by the Earl's news and now made ready for
action.

"Let them go," a small voice whispered into the stark silence.

And Gertrude's watchful gaze rested, like the Earl's and Sir
George's, on Lady Maud, whose dark, moody face had
unexpectedly transfigured into radiance. In her way too, Maud
had been suddenly jolted – to find her thick fog of hopelessness
dispersing.

"They shall be found," declared Sir George, his anger visibly rising. He shot a look at Edward Stanley and the cold glint of bitterness in his eyes conveyed a clear meaning: revenge!

"They shall certainly be found," Shrewsbury informed him with firm assurance, "but by my servants and under my protection." Again, his stern, but strained expression repressed Sir George's protests.

The Earl strode to the door and summoned William Crossland from the hall.

"You have recently come from Wingfield Manor?" he queried.

"Yes, my lord."

"Did you see any riders fleeing along your path?"

The servant reddened and blurted out, "I passed two riders heading for Matlock, sir, but it was too dark to tell who they were."

"Hm," grunted the Earl, "and you so well-known to Master John. Still, I shall give you another chance to see him – and this time, you will escort him to Wingfield!"

With that, the Earl marched decisively into the hall while the Countess, solicitous for more information, followed, whispering with William Crossland. The messenger's abashed look had not been lost on John's perceptive sister and now her thoughts ran on: knowing John, he will have taken Dorothy far away from Haddon ... knowing John ... but where?

Shrewsbury had already begun to issue his orders before Gertrude could interrupt him: some servants were to ride hard towards Wiverton, others towards John's Lincolnshire home at Uffington.

"Nay, my lord," she said, placing her hand on his arm, "even Uffington is too close to Vernon lands for complete safety. John has taken Dorothy north – to his old Yorkshire estates."

She nodded towards William Crossland, now apparently well recovered from his earlier discomfort, and a hint of a smile spread across her husband's face. "All the better," mused the Earl, "for in Yorkshire they are already under protection. How fortunate we are, my dearest lady, that your eldest brother is Lord President of the North!"

He rescinded his previous orders and addressed himself again to his messenger, "Well, man, you may speak plain now. Who *were* those two riders you passed?"

William Crossland bowed and then glanced furtively towards the parlour.

"My apologies, sir," he said in a low voice. "They were Master Manners' servants."

"Indeed? So you had to cloak the truth in there."

"I was trying to help Master Manners, my lord."

"Well, now you can, my friend," replied Shrewsbury, clapping him warmly on the shoulders. "Take Thomas Stringer with you and ride north with all possible speed. And when you find Master John and his lady, you must persuade them to return to Sheffield. There we shall all meet with them, to arrange their marriage openly."

So thought the Earl! But in the parlour meanwhile, Edward Stanley was asserting his views.

"A father's rights ..." he reminded Sir George.

"Leave them be!" intervened Maud. "Can't you see that Dorothy does not want you? And you," she rounded on Sir George, "need you still be so blind?"

She broke off, knowing her words were useless. The two men continued speaking above her, as if she was not there.

"Why do you hesitate?" challenged Stanley. "You who have such power!"

"Shrewsbury," muttered Sir George.

"What! Your Great Earl," scoffed the younger man.

"Aye, the Great Earl – who could make life very uncomfortable for me if he so wished."

"Huh!"

"You forget this involves his kinsman."

"I'll kill the scoundrel myself!"

Sir George looked away, ignoring the sharp cry from his wife. "God knows," he said, mastering his voice with difficulty, "my Lord Earl holds no firm authority over you. At least not yet!"

"Away, then," blustered Stanley. "To Matlock and beyond!" And the thin, uncompromising mouth curled upwards a little at the bearded corners as Sir George turned towards him again. He gave a swift bow and was gone, clattering out in great haste along the narrow passage to the gardens.

Maud peered cautiously into the hall and saw he had left unnoticed.

Oh, Dorothy, she thought with a sigh, I too wish I could flee.

She then heard Sir George call to her and she went back, head bowed, to his side, a sense of hopelessness engulfing her once more.

The grey light of morning found Dorothy and John well beyond Sheffield. They had slackened their pace slightly since leaving the town, and now the Pennine moors stirred all around them in vast billows towards the distant skyline.

John's face was rigidly alert, his senses sharpened by the danger and all the hardship of these past months. Strange, how he had grown accustomed to such a life. He was not sorry to see it go. No more roughened logs beneath his lonely head at night. From now on, soft pillows and feather beds would once more charm his sleep. And as for his young bride ...!

He glanced at the slender figure beside him and his expression immediately softened. Dorothy's face was flushed from the exertion of their ride, her eyes bright with all the hope of new life. With a high heart she had opened her entire spirit to these high moors because they signified her freedom – and freedom to her meant love. Even the wind seemed to welcome her as it ruffled and tore at her hair.

She returned John's glance and smiled – a young, eager, shining rush of deep joy. For a moment his own happiness turned to awe and it was with great reluctance that he roused his attention away from her to take in the scene around them. Pockets of snow still lay in numerous hollows and the heather-clad land itself was now lifting higher and higher against the sky as the rutted track ahead entered a steep descent. They were approaching the junction of two paths and very soon they would reach it; then he caught the sound they had been fearing most – the hurried gallop of horsemen approaching them. From which direction? His features set hard again, his hand rested reassuringly on the pistol at his belt. He thought he heard a shout, and in an instant his sword was drawn. Then silence closed over the pair in a seemingly deathly hush.

Instinctively, Dorothy guided her horse closer to John's, her eyes following his every move, her confidence in him unquestioning. Gingerly she rode forward with him, sitting straight and stiff in the saddle, as though she had been carved from the gritstone rocks above them.

When they neared the adjoining track, some of these rocks, jutting out, hid all but the meeting point from their view. Suddenly a call came from along that other path and two tousle-haired riders confronted them.

"Well met, sir!" panted William Crossland.

"Good God!" John cried, more harshly than he intended, but so menacing did he still feel, having braced himself for a fight. "What are you doing here?"

"My lord and lady send you greeting," the messenger went on.

"What do they want of us?" John had put his sword away, but his face stayed implacably sombre.

"They would help you all they can, sir, if only you will return with us to Sheffield. Today the Earl and Countess are travelling there, Mistress Vernon's family too, to settle your marriage openly."

John made no reply but, dismounting, spoke a few soft words to Dorothy in the voice he used for her alone. He lifted her down from her saddle, and though great still were his misgivings, he loosened their horses' girths, entrusting the servants with the task of holding their reins.

He put his arm then around her waist and together, the lovers ascended a little way to the shelter of a rocky outlier.

"What shall we do?" he asked. "Shall we return to a possible trap?" He held her still within the circle of his arm and briefly she leaned against him, thinking with pleasure how he always valued her opinion. How heartening this was after years of being overruled by her father!

"If we go on, I bring you only my willing body – sir!" she smiled, looking at him seductively out of the corners of her eyes.

"Enchantress!" he whispered, pulling her closer to him. The

brooding look had left his face and he was shaken with such a passion that he almost forced her against the sheer rock face.

She coyly placed a hand on his mouth. "But if we go back," she continued, "I will also bring you rich lands."

"Do we need rich lands, Dorothy?"

She shook her head. "But won't you accept them for our children?" she said.

He moved away from her a little, looking first at the track which would take them north and then at the Shrewsbury servants waiting patiently with the horses.

"John, the Earl was ever your friend," she went on.

"I have no quarrel with my Lord Earl," he replied.

"Or the Countess, your loving sister?"

"Dorothy, if the Countess, my loving sister, had helped me when I asked her, we could have wed long ago."

"I have no doubt of her sincerity towards us," said Dorothy in Gertrude's defence. "She is ... one of the kindest people I've ever met and I can't forget that."

John found himself smiling at this tribute to his sister. She had refused in her well-meaning way to help him once, it was true, but he had admitted himself that was long ago.

"We shall go back," he decided, after a pause. "Our ties with the Shrewsburys mean much to us both."

As they walked hand in hand back to the two servants, John called amiably to William Crossland, "Are we bound for the castle or the manor house, Will?"

"The manor house, sir," grinned the messenger. "You will find all things needful there and my Lord Earl hopes to sup with you this evening."

John was pleased to learn this. Of the two Shrewsbury residences at Sheffield, he far preferred the cosier manor house situated in parkland about two miles from the castle. The Earl himself had directed that Dorothy and John should be lodged there, and the other chief negotiators at the castle.

Shrewsbury arrived at the manor house promptly at supper-time, bringing with him Alice and Joan, and after their rapturous reunion with their mistress, he dined privately in his parlour with Dorothy and John.

"I expected to find you both fair spent," he observed, studying them with his usual grave gentleness.

"Love suits us, my lord," replied John blandly.

And the meal continued in an atmosphere of harmony. When at last they had finished, Shrewsbury remarked to his brother-in-law, "Your elopement was well-planned, John. One erstwhile suitor, Sir Edward Stanley, took his drunken squire in pursuit of your servants."

The look of happiness died on John's face.

"What became of my men?" he asked uneasily.

"Fortunately, nothing," replied the Earl. "They were already clean away."

"Erstwhile, you said," John reminded him, moving to stand behind Dorothy's chair. "And what of the raucous knight?"

"Ah, to complicate matters further, I sent some of my men after him."

"And?"

"And somehow they conducted him back to Haddon, where Sir George, Lady Maud and I exchanged words with him – before his brisk and huffy departure."

Shrewsbury gazed kindly at Dorothy as she mouthed the name, "Lady Maud?" in astonishment.

"Yes, my dear. Tis partly thanks to her that Sir Edward makes no further claim on you. You must forgive me if I quote his own blunt words." He looked at John again with mild amusement. "That you, sir, are more than welcome to Mistress Dorothy!"

Their faces turned towards each other, Dorothy and John dissolved into laughter and Shrewsbury allowed them their joyous moment before he raised his hand to signal, "Enough!"

He then continued, "The Countess and I have already undertaken some haggling on your behalf."

"We are much in your debt, my lord," said John.

"There will come a time, John, when I may be much in yours," answered the Earl with quiet authority. "I am afraid that Sir George still shows little enthusiasm for the match, but I shall ensure he comes to a compromise, however grudgingly, when we all assemble here in the morning."

After he had left his two guests in their congenial new surroundings, the Earl rode back to his castle.

Early the next day, John was about to leave his chamber when he heard the sound of youthful laughter outside his door, followed by a continuous flow of whispers and giggles moving some way up the corridor. Dorothy and her maid, could it be? He thought not, although they did often giggle together in corners. Then, as the solution came to him, he flung open the door and crept away stealthily after the culprits.

Two pairs of excited eyes were soon beaming up at him, but of course the whispering had stopped the minute they saw him.

"Uncle!" chorused Gilbert and Mary, and wobbled into the requisite bow and curtsey in delight.

"Good morning, niece and nephew," laughed John, making a flourishing bow. "And how secretive we look today!"

"Secret?" cried Gilbert. "There is no secret."

"You deceive me." The blue eyes twinkled as he grinned from one to the other. "I shall investigate this plot against me. And who will tell me about it? You, my little lady?"

"We would keep no secret from *you*, Uncle John," squeaked Mary, beginning to giggle again.

"I would wrest it from you were you not so pretty."

"As pretty as Mistress Dorothy?" The eight year old girl looked beyond him and waved her hand in a purely childlike expression of warmth as Dorothy came up to them.

After another round of bows and curtseys, Gilbert bawled, "You're going to marry Mistress Dorothy, aren't you, Uncle? I told you there was no secret."

And forgetting all etiquette, he tore down the stairs in front of the other three and noisily assured the first person he met, "He's going to marry her!"

"Is that so?" enquired the chill, flat voice of his godfather.

Dorothy, on hearing her father's voice, did not flinch, but placed her hand swiftly in John's and walked quietly beside him as they descended to the parlour.

"Your favourite godson has a somewhat hasty temperament, Sir George," they overheard the Earl saying.

"A man after my own heart!" exclaimed Sir George.

They found him looking down at the boy with obvious affection and even John could only envy his nephew on this occasion. Gilbert, though now ten years old, was still blissfully unaware of the adult storms and strife around him. To John's advantage, however, was the boy's open attachment to him. Gilbert's uninhibited chatter to Sir George had, so the Earl told John the previous day, contained many complimentary references to him and now 'Uncle John' wondered how much effect this had had on Dorothy's father.

When the children had returned to their nurse and the formal greetings were over, three men and three women gathered tensely around the Earl's table.

"My Lord Earl speaks highly of you," said Sir George gruffly, giving his would-be son-in-law a hard and frowning stare curiously mingled with embarrassment.

John inclined his head in reply, his cold, steady gaze noting the continued displeasure towards him. Sir George then cast a venomous glance at his daughter, but failed to make any impression on her.

Oh, how that Vernon temper craves to burst its restraining bonds! thought John wryly. But the Shrewsburys are here this time.

Sir George began clearing this throat with the exaggerated thoroughness which John remembered from before had preceded jibes of disapproval. But then the Earl stepped in to open the proceedings. At the mention of Dorothy's name, John turned his eyes, bright and adoring towards her and then glanced up in surprise at the look of doting approval he saw between Gertrude and ... Dorothy's stepmother!

So, Lord Shrewsbury had been right about the aid of this lady. The King of the Peak stood alone, not only over the question of his daughter's marriage, but also now in this room. His chair screeched along the floor as he thrust it, vacant, towards the table and then Dorothy watched in amazement as her father paced rapidly up and down. Back and forth, to and fro he veered with all the force of some westerly gale. And all the while he did so, the negotiations went painfully ahead with

the Earl in command at the helm. He reeled off a list of manors
to be settled on Dorothy:

"Haddon?"

"I shall bequeath it to my wife."

"Aylestone?"

"Aye, Doll can have that – when I'm dead."

His sheer energy of movement created a draught past
Gertrude when he said that and indeed, as the number of
Dorothy's properties grew, the Countess became increasingly
weary of Sir George's ceaseless prowling and at last gave vent to
her own feelings.

"Do you begrudge your daughter a little happiness?" she
demanded of him. "I for one think that is long overdue."

She smiled then apologetically at her brother, adding more
gently, "Tis my prayer now that the sorrows you have both
known are behind you and that your life together will be all you
wish for."

Dorothy and John responded to her with murmurs of
grateful agreement. Grateful, because Sir George, with his
habitual courtesy towards her, appeared at least to listen to her
words; but his expression as he stopped near Gertrude
disclosed a man whose tatters of patience had now been
unbearably rent.

His anger exploded at Dorothy, "All right, marry him! And
have your lands. But do not think I will celebrate your wedding
at Haddon, or that I will attend. You can be married at
Aylestone. It is far enough away."

The girl heard him out with a gallant self-possession,
thought Gertrude. And then Dorothy's new sense of stability
manifested itself again when her hand reached out slowly, but
surely to brush against her father's as he passed her to return to
his seat.

But as the rejoicing and congratulations followed his heated
tirade, Sir George merely slumped down in his chair, looking
suddenly an old and very tired man.

EIGHT

The manor of Aylestone lay on the edge of Leicester Forest, some two miles south of the town itself. Leicester was now a poor place which had once known better days, and a disastrous storm there had recenlty wrought havoc.

In complete contrast was the merry cavalcade which rode through its forlorn streets as March of 1563 gave way to a softer April.

For Dorothy, Aylestone had always seemed a happy place. A place of childhood picnics in the green refreshed shade of forest clearings. A place of springtime celebrations when the nearby Easter Hare Hunt dispelled Black Annis from the forest for yet another year.

Black Annis, the local goddess of winter who was said to haunt the forest! There had been times when Dorothy thought this evil spirit had gone far beyond the bounds of Leicester Forest in order to torment her. But now, as they rode across the ancient bridge and past the church towards Aylestone Manor, she could hardly believe her own happiness, how by some miracle she had been brought to these moments of rich fulfilment when less than six months before her life had been an empty and cruel mockery. She knew she would always cherish her happiness and try to preserve it, for she of all people had learnt that it could never be taken for granted.

And in the end too, her friends had fought for her happiness. Friends which in one case she had not even known existed, for despite her father's conspicuous absence, he had been placated enough to allow Lady Maud to attend.

How quiet, how peaceful this wedding would be compared with Margaret's, or the lavishness of Maud's for that matter. Dorothy was almost overwhelmed by the transformation of her stepmother into a lively, pleasant young woman who was after all not much older than herself.

The spring sunshine cast a living golden light across the bridal chamber, as though matching the mood of those within.

And Maud tended Dorothy almost lovingly as she anointed her with a fragrant essence of amber, helped to dress her in the gown of white brocade and combed her glossy hair, leaving it to flow loose down to her waist. With Alice and Joan in attendance, she proudly set a circlet of pearls on the girl's head, a circlet of pearls which she had presented as her own special gift.

The looking-glass reflected back to them two sparkling, shining images.

"We have been living under a cloud," confided Dorothy.

"A miserable, heavy cloud," agreed this new friendly Maud. "I have passed my youth tied to an old man. I am happy for you that you will not only marry a young man, but also one of your own choice."

Dorothy pressed her hand.

"Last time, I had no choice," continued Maud. "But next time, if there is a next time, I too will marry to please myself."

"Next time!" joked Dorothy. "I rejoice to have reached this time!"

"He is a fine man and comes of good family."

"I shall of course adopt his religion."

"Ah, religion!" sighed Maud's reflection. "There too I believe you have chosen well."

"But your family ..."

"They held back your happiness once, Dorothy. They will never do so again. Nor would I allow them to with me. Besides, the days of Catholicism are numbered. It will probably wither away and die, though I should not speak thus with your father."

Strong words on the day of Dorothy's wedding! But in after years when the bride herself thought of this day, she saw it bathed in that rich golden light, a bright yellow nimbus encircling her precious memories.

She remembered the warmth of all those in the procession which accompanied her to the church, its broach spire rising above the trees, its weather-vane glinting in the sunlight. And in that glowing light they walked through a small gateway and along the dancing shade of a tree-lined path towards the porch, where John was already waiting for her with some of his own kin. John, dressed in white and gold of the finest cloth, his handsome face shining. He looked magnificent, and for a moment she felt humility that she had dared to expect love from him.

Then the faint scent of amber restored her self-esteem. Amber from the white doeskin gloves which they had given to each other as love tokens.

They stood close together in the church porch. There was a minister called William Heathcot who spoke in the strong, familiar accent of Derbyshire. There were vows, repeated first by the deep, resounding voice on her right-hand side. Then her own voice drifted out:

"I, Dorothy, take thee, John, to my wedded husband, to have and to hold, from this day forward, for better for worse, for richer for poorer, in sickness and in health ..."

There were tears in her eyes and a stirring of great affection at the gentleness with which he placed the ring on her finger. There were prayers and blessings, then the iron-hinged door was opened and they all entered the church. Again, her impressions were of space and light, of sunbeams streaming down on them through painted glass, and of their hands joined together as now at last were their lives.

What a different bride was Dorothy from the fearful Maud on her wedding night! Then the girl's stepmother had submitted like a doll with no life of her own to being undressed and led to the marriage bed. And in the morning she had awoken to find herself alone once more, weeping, and shivering with a cold that it seemed nothing could ever warm.

But now, away from Haddon and away from Sir George, the two young women sang softly together while Dorothy was in her turn being prepared for bed. Their song was one they would never be allowed to sing in his presence, for although it had first appeared around Haddon Hall, it had been inspired by Dorothy's elopement.

It happened between March and May-Day,
When wood-buds wake which slumbered late,

When hill and valley grow green and gaily
And every wight longs for a mate.
When lovers sleep with an open eye-lid
Like nightingales on the orchard tree,
And sorely wish they had wings for flying
So they might with their true love be.

And very soon Dorothy would "with her true love be". She had been honourably and respectably married to him, yet she knew that throughout the area around Haddon the story of her elopement would always linger.

She had no qualms about that, she had no qualms about John, or the joys of bodily closeness she was about to discover. The hot wine had gone to her head a little and she was dizzy with excitement, dizzy with the heights of happiness she was now so near to achieving.

Dorothy had been disrobed behind a screen of curtains and beyond this, she could hear John talking to his companions while they divested him of his clothes.

In a minute, the curtains parted and her ladies filed quietly out, murmuring light-heartedly as they preceded the gentlemen attendants. They closed the door behind them on a world which held Dorothy and John alone.

He watched her tenderly as she stepped from behind the curtains, bestowing on him her wistful, but loving smile. With a rush of deep and fierce longing, she stretched out her arms towards him and when he readily caught her hands, their eyes met too without fear or striving.

"By God's precious soul," he whispered, "I shall love you till I die."

So great was the haze of her enchantment that before she knew, she was lying in bed beside him. And if at first she quivered, through every fibre of her body, at the touch of his light embrace, after that she clung to him while his arms closed hungrily round her. Dorothy had nothing but dreams with which to compare the ecstasy of their union, this total giving of themselves unto each other. His tenderness had evoked in her a passion to match his own, so that a blissful new dimension was added to their love.

They stayed at Aylestone Manor for three more days and nights, during which time they received many intimations of goodwill, whether from the village women and children who had thronged round them with gifts and heartily wished them well, or from John's relatives, with their earnest requests for visits.

"I'm convinced I am dreaming," said Dorothy, "and that I shall never, ever wake up again."

"Too late anyway," teased John. "You're caught!"

But sure enough, this dream-like quality persisted and he, overjoyed that all secrecy and misunderstanding had now been cleared, moved fast in accepting these welcome invitations. And although he always took pains to consult her, she felt as though she was floating on air after him and never quite catching up.

She did, however, manage to write a note of gentle affection to her new sister-in-law, Gertrude. Before long they were to see the Shrewsbury's again, visit the Earl of Rutland at Belvoir Castle and John's Nottinghamshire cousin at Annesley.

"Tell me about Wiverton," she pleaded.

"It is my home," said John, "though I but lease it from my cousin, George Chaworth."

And he motioned her to the table, where he sat down and smoothed out a blank sheet of paper. Picking up his quill pen, he began to draw with vigorous strokes a plan of Wiverton Hall. She watched him, fascinated, as the gatehouse appeared, then the buildings around two courtyards, the gardens around the site of an old Norman keep and the surrounding moat. And all this in the centre of a wooded park with the little river Smite nearby.

"I have heard," she said, leaning contentedly against his shoulder, "that Belvoir is a green and fertile country, full of fair meadows and soaring church spires."

He glanced sideways and kissed her. "It sounds as though you too are ready to go home," he said.

"Yes, John," she answered quietly. "I am more than ready to face our new life."

Engrossed in their future, their hearts were now eagerly

turned to that moated manor house in the Vale of Belvoir, where for the time being at least, their life together lay.

PART III: 1565-68

'Her second match she made by her own choice
Pleasing herself, who others pleased before.
Her ears she stopped from all dissuaders' voice,
Who did her tender wealth and goods great store.
With honour great, which both she did refuse
And one of meaner state herself did choose.'

From the epitaph of Lady Maud,
North Cadbury, Somerset

The mud-spattered homecoming after a days hawking

Dorothy appeals to Thomas to remain loyal to Queen Elizabeth

NINE

September had come, and there was an air of mourning around Haddon Hall.

"My cloud has lifted at last," declared Maud.

Margaret looked slightly askance at her as they stepped beneath the old archway in the course of their afternoon walk.

"The carvings!" mused Dorothy. "At least they are still here." And there they were, the G.V. and M.V. she had seen so many times before, with the words GOD SAVE THE VERNON. "Alas, the Vernon day is done."

"He was a tyrant," Maud went on.

"My lady!" exclaimed Margaret. "I pray you, do not speak ill of his memory."

"I could hardly do so when he was alive."

"You are over-wrought, you must try to rest."

"I never felt better!"

"Peace, ladies, peace!" implored Dorothy. Her voice faltered as she addressed Maud more softly. "Dear lady, you are right," she said sympathetically, "but one day, you too will think of him as I do. I remember only the warmth behind his tyranny and that he was so full of life. He filled every corner of Haddon with his own great abundance of life. It seems strangely empty without him."

Maud smiled gratefully at her. There was a bond between them now, and they had met often since Dorothy's marriage. Only Dorothy understood how misery had dulled Maud's heart and mind, how buoyant her sense of confidence now that time was over. Dorothy, who had battled so hard for her own happy marriage and delightfully been proved right. Sir George had been totally reconciled to her in the end. It was natural she should grieve for his death.

"They are together again now, the holders of these initials," Maud comforted.

"Yes," replied Dorothy, and then went on in an attempt to

include Margaret, "Our parents have a splendid tomb."

"'Tis worthy of them," said Margaret suavely.

The ladies returned to the parlour, where John Manners and Thomas Stanley were in lively debate about some clauses in Sir George's will. They would be business partners for some weeks yet, Dorothy smiled to herself, for they had been appointed along with Maud and the other named executors to administer the will. Whatever their differences, both men were conscientious and made an effort to be friends, but while this chance of co-operation between them was most welcome to Dorothy, in no way could it alleviate the gap left by her father.

Even so, she realized that a new longing had begun to work against her grief – a new need to fill this dear old house with life again. With a pack of healthy children, her maternal instincts suggested: *her* children, whom she had dreamed of so long ago! She was with child now, and though she loved her present home, Wiverton would never belong to her and John. Nor, she reflected with a certain sadness, would Haddon be theirs for many years, because Sir George had left it to Maud for her lifetime and only after that would it revert to his heirs.

Despite this, Dorothy knew without questioning or reasoning that Haddon was part of her and, as the early autumn progressed, she took every opportunity to wander around her childhood home, sauntering dreamily through some parts and with a wealth of nostalgia through others.

"I can hardly bear to leave here this time," she confided, during one of her journeyings, to Maud.

"You have so many memories."

"And hopes," she added.

"What hopes?"

"How I long to see this place sparkle again," said Dorothy. "And changes, I would make many changes. The long gallery, the gardens …"

"If I had the power to grant you Haddon right now, Dorothy, I would do so," Maud assured her.

"You do not wish to keep Haddon?"

"No," came the resolute reply. "I seek only happiness now."

"And love?" Dorothy's face brightened.

"And love," echoed Maud, pressing her hand on Dorothy's arm. "There must be some way we can help each other. If only there was a way."

If only!

But they parted company along a dark, narrow corridor and to Dorothy it seemed just then like a tunnel with no guiding light at the end. She drifted on alone, finding solace in the return of her daydreams, fanciful though they may be.

She would like to see the nursery refurbished of course and replace some old toys which had so long lain idle. Her nephew was its current occupant, and she played with him there whenever possible.

And yet her own children Dorothy had always pictured playing by the bridge. Of all her favourite old haunts, this was one she would never change, she thought, as she lingered down there with John one day.

"The scene of my most poignant memories," she remarked to him with wonder.

"The scene now of your most vivid hopes, I believe," he ventured with some amusement.

Dorothy looked at him a little startled. Were they so much at one that he could sense her innermost thoughts?

"You know me through and through," she smiled.

"And I care about your dream."

"Tis your dream too," she murmured and for a while they stood silently in each other's arms. She understood their silence; they were often silent in their deepest joys together.

Strolling together through the gardens, however, they found plenty to discuss.

"These yew trees shall one day be clipped anew," he decided.

"Into different shapes?"

"The shapes of both our family crests."

"The peacock and the boar are proud creatures," replied Dorothy, "but their blood has mingled gently."

He placed his hand lightly on her stomach.

"*Pour y parvenir*," she continued, "I like your family motto."

"To get there?"

"But will we ever get here?" she sighed.

"I'm sure we will," he affirmed.

She felt elated by his answer. Perhaps Maud had found a way? And there *was* Maud, beckoning to them from the garden terrace below. In her enthusiasm, Dorothy sped forward, accidentally losing her footing as she raced down the steps towards her. Suddenly the ground had tipped over into a vast expanse of sky and the steps were hitting her back like hammer-blows, as she plummeted to the bottom, screaming.

She landed in a dazed heap and opened her eyes on a swimming world, a myriad of anxious faces and voices seeming near, then far away. Bruised and badly shaken, she was conscious of being helped up to her feet, of limping stiffly for a few yards, then being lifted with ease into a pair of strong and loving arms. "To bed," "to rest," were the words now hammering through her head. But sleep, though she greatly wished for it, stubbornly refused to be enticed. Night came like a pall over her in the huge bed, and under its darkness, the shadows played tricks with her mind. Suddenly a searing pain shot through her and she let out an agonizing cry.

John caught her firmly at once. "Sweetheart, what is it?"

"I know not," she sobbed, then doubled up in his arms.

Soon afterwards she did know. The physician had done all he could. She lay on her pillows exhausted, her pale face staring apologetically at John through a misty curtain of tears. She had lost their child; she felt she had failed him. But from the expression on his face, she knew he did not blame her.

Her sense of loss was overpowering. So many deaths within her recent memory. First, two of John's brothers from the plague, then Alice at peace in her sleep. And then, after a short illness, the King of the Peak himself. But in losing her unborn child, it was as though part of herself had died.

She was vaguely aware of John, his face white and drawn, yet seeming once more to swim towards her, his hands gripping hers trying to comfort and reassure her. But somehow the white of his face and the dark of his hair were blurring together into wavering shades of grey and there was a roaring of rushing water in her ears. She passed into a fitful darkness and when she eventually came out of it, she could hear voices whispering above her. Now there were two blurred faces keeping vigil, where before there had only been one.

"She is coming to herself," said Maud with relief.

John called her name gently, several times. She heard herself groan in response. Instinctively her arms reached up to him and she felt his lips pressed against hers.

"Is it dark still?" she asked muzzily.

"Again!" he answered, smiling. "You've slept the day through." Dorothy looked at him in disbelief, then noticed the anxiety and tiredness meeting her gaze. "Yours was a restless and very troubled sleep," he added. "You cried out many times."

"I was dreaming badly."

"Of what?"

"Of the bridge and of the river," she said slowly. "Of children playing there, our children, and we were with them. But suddenly a great black creature swooped down on us, blotting out the sun." For an instant she shook with terror as the full shock of nightmare returned. "When it spoke, it had an evil voice and laughed at us and mocked us and told us to begone, for we would never have any children and never belong here, and ..." She drew a sharp breath. "It was but a dream," she whispered.

"I hope it never torments you again," said Maud kindly. "Now, more than ever, I am convinced we should help each other."

"I cannot see how," began Dorothy weakly.

"But you will do presently, when you are stronger."

Dorothy looked up in her stepmother's direction, saw her, but did not really register Maud's expression till afterwards. Her consciousness was still too crowded with emotions which cast her down – though she believed she had detected a smile in the Lady of Haddon's voice.

Another day went by, another night, and when Dorothy awoke late the next morning, she was glad to find the sun shining on her face.

John bent over her from the bedside and she feigned an

outraged grimace. "Are *you* still here?" she greeted him. "I thought you had work to do."

He hooted with mock indignation. "There's gratitude for you, my lady!" he quipped at Maud.

Dorothy, her body suddenly taut, tried to sit up when she realized that Maud was also with them, but John pushed her gently back against her pillows.

"I'm stronger now," she asserted.

"So I see," he grinned, resuming his seat.

Then Maud came to her and took her hand. "How I wish for a marriage such as yours!" she murmured.

"Are you going to tell me now how we can help each other?"

"I am indeed. What I have to say concerns us all, for I think you know that these goods and lands which your father left me are no compensation for the emptiness in my heart. I would willingly cast them all to the winds in return for a happy marriage."

And in that moment, Maud was almost childlike in the way she frowned down at her own plain band of gold, while admiring Dorothy's wedding ring, for on it were engraved two tiny hands clasped together, supporting a tiny crowned heart. Symbols of love, what more could she want! A motto of her very own, for inside Dorothy's ring were the words:

> *Wear me out, love shall not waste*
> *For love beyond all time is placed.*

"Next time, I too will have a posy ring," she sighed.

"But when will this next time be?" asked Dorothy.

"Soon," flushed Maud. "It may be very soon. But even sooner, I fear I shall be greatly at odds with my family."

"Why so?"

"Religion is the first reason – and then of course my intention to give up my share of the Vernon lands."

"Is there no other way?"

"No. For if I do this, I shall then be free to marry my choice. And you, since you already own much land in these eastern counties, would almost certainly gain the Derbyshire estates. Those in Staffordshire would go to Margaret."

"And the Derbyshire manors include Haddon," smiled Dorothy.

"Exactly."

"Whatever happens when you face your family, you may count on our support," said John. Dorothy agreed. After all, they had both known their differences with her relatives. Even now, she still chafed over Margaret's surprisingly slow acceptance of John into their family, though Thomas, thankfully, had proved more generous.

"I rejoice in your support," Maud cried with pleasure, "for I know it will carry much weight."

Dorothy sat up, yawned and fell back against her pillows with a sigh of contentment. Physically, she still felt very weak, but strangely enough the world was suddenly full of delightful new prospects for all of them. The legal process would take time of course. There would have to be an inquisition post mortem, but how readily she could share Maud's irrepressible certainty that all would go well.

John grinned at her and pinched her cheeks. This was more like the Dorothy he knew.

But when Maud told them whom her 'choice' was, even Dorothy and John were briefly at a loss.

"Sir Francis Hastings?" mused John. "You mean Huntingdon's young brother?"

"The very same."

"My God! No wonder you'll have to give up your lands."

"But I thought," said Dorothy, "that one of those brothers had already married into the Port family."

"Yes," answered Maud, "and he is the only Catholic amongst them. Sir Francis is, like the Earl of Huntingdon ..."

"An extreme and zealous Protestant if ever there was one!" stated John very quietly.

"I would have wed him years ago had I been allowed."

And Maud was clearly determined to do so – this time.

When her family assembled with her in the great chamber a few days later, Maud stood before them the very picture of decision.

"Have you taken leave of your senses?" enquired Nicholas Longford, her brother. "Your husband has left you more than well provided for."

"We could arrange another advantageous marriage for you," said her mother. "Another *Catholic* marriage."

"Like the last one?" retorted Maud. "Nay, I have learnt my lesson – and learnt it the hard way thanks to you two."

Lady Port affected tears. "How dare you speak to me thus? Your own mother!"

"I dare many things now that I am free," answered Maud bitterly.

"But you were content," said her sister.

"How do you know?"

"Well, you conducted yourself with dignity as Sir George's wife. And he loved you. He said so himself."

"Mere words!" flashed Maud. "Do you know how much I have suffered?"

"Nonsense," returned her brother. "You must renounce your marriage hopes and accept the will as it stands."

"Because you tell me to?"

Her eyes blazed as hot as his, so undaunted did she face him.

"You have long prepared yourself for this, haven't you – my lady?" he taunted.

"How clever you are," she applauded coldly.

"Which is more than we can say for you! We'll see what pressure the other executors can bring to bear on you."

That pressure, had it not been for the steadfast loyalty of John Manners towards her, she knew would have been enormous. But John, by his mere presence, was a man who could command respect. And what was more, he had a powerful relative who was keenly interested in the proceedings. The Earl of Shrewsbury may have left Haddon soon after the funeral, but the sooner his brother- in-law became its Lord, the better, as far as he was concerned.

Dorothy, still recuperating from her miscarriage, was tense with anticipation as she kept to her bed. Yet an inner voice was calming her, and telling her to trust in the single-mindedness of her stepmother who, backed up by the strength of John, would stoically refuse to be ruffled.

But the waiting seemed endless before the familiar footsteps sounded outside her door.

She sat bolt upright, firing questions at them in her eagerness before they had fully entered the room.

"All is well," John smilingly reassured her.

And as for the expression on Maud's face! "Victory as well as mutual gain," she announced breathlessly.

The two women hugged each other.

"But what of your family?" murmured Dorothy.

"I shall enjoy riches of a vastly different kind, I informed them and my co-executors," Maud said. "Then my brother retorted, 'Well then, you have sealed your fate. We wash our hands of you'." She assumed a deep voice in imitation of him and strode manfully up and down, making impatient gestures with her hands. "My mother and sister did the same," her usual voice continued. "I care not! From now onwards, I shall live way above the clouds!"

The inquisition post mortem was then a mere formality. After a pleasant sojourn at Wiverton, Dorothy and John rode back to Derbyshire in order to attend it. And so, as 1565 wound into the eighth year of Elizabeth's reign, Lady Maud resigned all her interests in Sir George's property and her share of the lands was divided between his two co-heiresses, Dorothy and Margaret. In accordance with their stepmother's prediction, Margaret, already the owner of Tong Castle, received all the Staffordshire estates and Dorothy the much-loved Derbyshire lands.

As heiress of Haddon now, and sooner, so much sooner than she had once thought possible, Dorothy had regained her bloom. True, she and John would not actually possess it until Maud remarried and the lady would continue to live here till then, but that was no hindrance to Dorothy's high spirits.

The day after the inquisition was marked by another of her extensive tours around her old home – her new home! When she eventually returned to their apartments, she quietly pushed open the door and saw John sitting at the table, writing. She advanced into the room, trying to look haughty, moving deliberately very close to him. His hand reached for hers and caressed it. Then laughing, she flung her arms around his neck.

"What are you writing?" she asked after a moment.

"A letter to the Shrewsburys, to tell them of yesterday's outcome."

She released him and sat down beside him, and some minutes later she scanned the completed effort.

"How this will gladden the Earl and Countess!" she enthused.

"And no regrets that through you, Dorothy, Haddon now passes out of the Vernons' name?"

"After almost four hundred years. Tis a long time!" she mused. "But a new era soon begins, John, and this house could not be in better care than yours."

He cupped her face in his hand and kissed her.

"We must return to Wiverton for the winter," he told her. "I fear still for your health and the Derbyshire snows will not help you."

"I can leave here with a peaceful heart now," she replied.

And she must be well enough to give her husband an heir, she knew. But she was young yet, only twenty, and time was still on her side.

Life flowed along contentedly at Wiverton, which in winter was warm and cosy compared with houses on higher ground. The following March blew mild and occasionally wet across the fertile green flatness around, and Dorothy, standing with John one day before the parapet of the gatehouse, reflected how happy they had been in this place. Beneath them stretched a broad expanse of Nottinghamshire, and Leicestershire towards Belvoir Castle. She exclaimed with wonder when he pointed out to her that grey clouds were massing once more over the blue ridge of hills on the horizon and against them a rainbow had suddenly arched up in its brilliant, trembling colours.

She watched it spellbound until it faded. What if their tranquil life together should also become a memory? Their return to Haddon would not be without its challenges ... and yet, *together*, Dorothy assured herself, glancing at John, its new Lord and Lady would meet them. She put her hands on his shoulder, propping her chin on them pertly as she looked up at him.

"Will you miss here when you see rainbows over Derbyshire hills?" she asked.

"New life, new adventure," he said simply.

Adventure? She wholeheartedly agreed with him and soon afterwards her spirits were soaring when they travelled on Lady Day to Aylestone. From there they honoured an invitation to visit Maud at the Huntingdons' town house in Leicester, where she introduced them to her youthful betrothed. Sir Francis was touchingly devoted to Maud, so Dorothy noted with pleasure, and what a contrast from Sir George!

On April 1st at Aylestone, a wild enchanted mood overcame both Dorothy and John. A mood born of the magic of springtime and the promise of the years ahead. They called for horses, then galloped off into the forest until they came to a hidden brook. They reined in, carefree, amorous, when a sense of happy mischief seemed to shake her like the wind.

"Look to your saddle, love," she warned, trying hard to appear unhurried.

And John, believing her, immediately dismounted. She heard him pose her a question, then caught his knowing laugh. Too late! The chase was on. But Dorothy exhorting, encouraging her horse, leaning forward on his neck, had already covered much ground.

The forest resounded to their horses' hooves, thudding hither and thither amid the rustling, sun-flecked shade. Then the thought suddenly struck John that he could no longer hear her horse. She must be nearby. Where was she hiding? Well, doubtless he would soon find out. And when he did ...!

He continued into a clearing and there he saw her horse, riderless as he had expected. But Dorothy? His heart sank when he spotted her fragile body lying motionless in the grass. He dismounted again, this time with a frantic urgency, and after he had wrapped the reins of both horses around a low-growing branch, he all but flung himself down beside her. He slid an arm beneath her and with the other he touched her face. An involuntary giggle escaped from her, much to his heartfelt relief.

"I won!" she happily informed him as her eyes opened laughing and bright.

"April fool!" he pretended to growl. "The victory is yours, sweetheart, but the prize I intend to be mine!"

Desire overwhelmed him in a rising tide as he pushed away her restraining hand. Even as he did so, she felt the sharp pressure of her wedding ring and was fleetingly reminded of the posy which Maud had decided for hers.

"In thee, my choice, I do rejoice," she whispered, closing her arms around him.

TEN

Dorothy and John spent the summer of 1566 at Uffington, the manor near Stamford which he leased from the Earl of Rutland.

With them they had taken their proudest and best-trained hawks, for often they rode out across the fenlands to a full day's sport, their falcons perched belled and hooded upon their gloves, returning home exhilarated, their feathered catch slung limp across their saddles.

John took his genial brother-in-law hawking when the Stanleys visited them in August. But Dorothy, as lady of the manor, felt obliged to stay at home with Margaret. And so, on a grey unseasonal day the two sisters found themselves embroidering together while Edward capered around his parents' apartments on his hobby horse, pretending to be like his father.

"You are proud of your papa," smiled Dorothy.

"Yes," grinned the boy, "and I will also grow big and strong." He put down the hobby horse and stretched his arms up in the air as high as he could. "I wish I could go out riding," he told her after that.

"Well, you can't. It's raining," said his mother.

Edward looked downcast, not knowing what to play next. He

slouched towards the window and grudgingly stared at the rain.

"I can't see Uncle William yet," he grumbled.

"He *is* coming today," Dorothy reassured him.

"He'll get very wet."

"Is it still raining?"

He nodded his head and knelt on the window seat, looking very thoughtful. When Dorothy went over to join him, he clambered happily onto her knee.

"Tell a story," he suddenly demanded.

She had been expecting that. And the knowledge that Uncle William was coming to see them from Gautby had filled her head with stories. For Uncle William, Sir William Tailbois, that was, her mother's brother, was an old Lincolnshire clergyman with a whole host of stories to tell. Her mind wandered briefly back to her childhood, to those tales she had never tired of hearing – Beauty and the Beast, Jack the Giant-Killer, Tom Thumb. And when she was older, nearly a woman, he had told her often about Bessie Blount, her famous aunt who had been the mistress of King Henry VIII and even borne him a son.

She decided, however, that her nephew was still perhaps too young to hear about Bessie Blount, and so as the rain continued to pour, "once upon a time" merged into a long and curious rambling about giants and beanstalks, and small boys called Jack and Tom, and a beautiful lady and an ugly beast, interspersed by numerous questions from the child.

"I think you are too sleepy for any more story," she said at last.

"*Not* too sleepy," he protested drowsily. "Story not finished." She had not taken long to realize, watching him and catching Margaret's calm, approving gaze, that the content of the story did not matter much. What he wanted was her nearness, her attention and the sound of her voice, for he loved her almost as much as his papa, so he said. She loved him too and hugged him suddenly, impulsively, wishing that he was hers.

"Why, lady, are you crying?" asked Edward, blinking up at her.

"'Tis nothing, little one."

She tossed her head to shake off the sadness that she had no children of her own, her outward movement making him laugh. She repeated the gesture, determinedly laughing with him, then bent her head closer so he could wipe away a tear.

"You are a good boy," she whispered.

"Was Beauty a good boy – in the story?"

"No, Beauty was a lady. Now I know you were asleep!"

"Was Beauty a queen then?"

"If you like. She can be a queen in our story."

"My papa writes letters to the Queen," he said chirpily.

"To Queen Elizabeth?"

"Lisbet?" The child looked at her blank. "No! Queen Mary," he added, though his voice seemed far away as Dorothy saw a rare frown cross Margaret's face..

"Edward, that's enough!" said Margaret Stanley firmly. He asked her why, but she countered by removing him from his dazed and speechless aunt's knee.

"No, no!" he wailed, trying to cling to Dorothy's skirts. "I want to stay with her." But calling his nurse from the ante-room, Margaret thrust the indignant boy at her and he was bundled, howling, out of the room.

"Children!" shrugged Margaret nonchalantly, returning to her embroidery.

"Yes, children!" cried Dorothy with sudden force. She got up from the window seat. "An innocent child, a babe. How was he to know that what he said was wrong?"

"My son reminds me of others in our family," observed Margaret coolly. "Tact is not his strongest asset."

Her sister shot her a dagger glance. Had those words been meant to hurt? Well, hurt they certainly did, and from Dorothy the storm now broke.

"Have no fear," she retorted bitterly, "your secret is safe with me. But what of others? If this news about your husband should fall into the wrong hands, my dear, *dear* sister, then where would your precious Thomas be? In gravest danger! And how can you sit there with your stitchwork so smug and unconcerned. Will you stitch when he goes to the Tower?"

"The Queen of Scots is riding high," said Margaret. "Why

shouldn't Thomas write to her and assure her of his friendship?"

"I do not know what you mean – riding high."

"She has a son now, an heir."

"So?"

"That strengthens her claim to the English throne. If Elizabeth were to die ..."

"Elizabeth is not dead!" exclaimed Dorothy loyally. "God grant Her Majesty long life, then we shall have no need of her successors."

"If Elizabeth were to die," insisted Margaret, "Mary would be our next Queen. She wishes only for Elizabeth to acknowledge that fact. And Thomas, amongst others, heartily supports her claim."

"Thomas should have more care."

"Well, you tell him that. And see where your warning gets you!"

Dorothy flounced away from her, more tears welling up in her eyes, a weakness she wished she could conquer. But this was not the first time she had felt fear for the safety of Thomas and Margaret, and that instance before, she recalled, had involved the Queen of Scots. Since those days a rift, ever-widening and deeply disturbing, had arisen between her and Margaret, yet she could not think of her sister without unwilling love struggling within her. There was so much to remember from their long-lost years of affection.

She looked round at Margaret. "I will talk with Thomas," she said.

Margaret acceded to her viewpoint with a casual, "If you must." She then went on to say. "Since you know so much already, you shall at least know the rest. Queen Mary replied to Thomas that through him she hopes to win over the Duke of Norfolk, his cousin, to her cause. Also the Earls of Derby and Shrewsbury, whom she believes to be of the old religion, which she intends to restore in England."

Dorothy bit her lip. "She is wrong about Shrewsbury."

"Shrewsbury? *His* religious tendencies I know, but how good of you to remind me, you being one of his kin now." There was a note of accusation, of deceptively-veiled contempt in her low, smooth voice.

So, my sister, you still resent that, thought Dorothy, almost stung into another fury. Sadly, it seemed that their rift was not a passing phase, for they had married men of different ideas and beliefs, of different loyalties to different Queens ...

Dorothy's musings and the sounds of bustling activity in the courtyard below had taken her back to the window.

"Riders?" speculated Margaret, coming to stand at her side.

They looked down simultaneously and Dorothy breathed a silent sigh of gratitude, for Uncle William had just arrived from Gautby. Uncle William, this favourite companion from their childhood. A part of her ached now for those happy days and how appropriate was such a feeling, she thought, here in the native county of their mother.

Dorothy, followed by Margaret, hastened to greet the newcomer, hoping that the stories they could share with him would bring them a little closer.

The rain had stopped at last and water lay in pools across the sodden flatness of the fens. The air was alive with sonorous bells and cries of "Aloft, aloft!", "Well flown!"

The gentlemen, with their spaniels, were following the flight of their hawks on foot, strong staffs helping them to negotiate the many ditches.

"Oh, now she takes her and strikes her down like a thunderbolt," called Thomas.

"She has struck ten pounds from me!" said John, reminding him of their betting.

They leapt across a ditch and soon afterwards came to another. Over went John, to be followed as he thought by Thomas. But an ominous-sounding crack was heard just before a heavy and duly cursed splash.

Incredulous, John swung round immediately. "What the ..."

He stopped short as his companion grinned up at him ruefully from the bottom of the ditch. "D'ye think this'll inspire a new fashion?" quipped Thomas, holding up in both hands his pole, which had completely snapped in two. He then stared

down at his breeches, pointing out their uniquely mud-caked
elegance.

"Ten pounds I owe you – twill be needed now!" laughed
John. He proceeded to effect the rescue, along with Thomas's
servant.

Thomas continued to make light of the incident with his
usual good humour, ensuring an atmosphere of merriment for
the rest of the day. Even greater was the laughter which he
enthusiastically encouraged when they presently arrived back at
the manor house.

Dearest Thomas, how I wish that was the only quagmire you
were falling into! thought Dorothy, teasing him with the others
at supper that evening.

She had a natural liking for the man – cared about him,
cared about what might happen to him …

He was beaming at her now through a haze of wine and
goodwill and though she spoke to him with a bubbling
cheerfulness, inwardly she felt a special need to discuss her
concern for him with someone.

And she was well aware she must judge carefully who that
someone might be. John? Perhaps on this occasion, no, she
thought, since he was ultra-loyal to Queen Elizabeth.

She would choose her moment to corner Thomas, of course,
although her ability to influence him was uncertain. And if she
should fail?

Uncle William! Then she could confide in him, she realized
on a happier note. He would respect her secrecy, so she would
not break her word to Margaret. He may have an old man's
tendency to look back on the past, but, as she had found out
before, his grasp on present events was remarkable.

But she had to see Thomas first. She made pretence of
showing the Stanleys round the garden and orchard the next
day and her mood towards her sister mellowed considerably
when Margaret, purring most affably at her hospitality,
endorsed yesterday's private agreement.

"Come, little one," she said. "Let us leave papa and Aunt
Dorothy to talk. I believe it is time for our reading."

Edward walked after her, pouting, each step dragging forth,

but eventually the inducement of "stories" persuaded him safely indoors.

Dorothy sauntered away with Thomas then, until she was confident they were out of earshot. From that moment their chit-chat changed from a pleasure to an irritation for her, so, characteristically she waded straight into her fears.

"I have heard about your ... correspondence with the Queen of Scots," she said slowly.

"And?"

"Thomas, you are playing a very dangerous game."

"Potentially dangerous," he corrected her. "Potentially brilliant too. When Her Majesty of Scotland becomes Her Majesty of England, she will remember her friends."

He sounds like his brother, she thought angrily for an instant and then pleaded with great feeling, "Thomas, you must tread warily – always."

"Sweet Doll," he murmured. "You know I can make you no such promise. We are two of a kind, you and I. There are times in our lives when we feel compelled to reach out for what we want, no matter what troubles we may have to face."

"I understand that."

"Yes, you married the man you loved, against all the odds. And nothing would have swayed you from your goal."

"Nothing," she agreed.

"I admired you for that," he said. "Your boldness, your tenacity. Would that you could feel the same for me."

"For you also wish to achieve your goal?"

"Aye. One day Mary Queen of Scots must succeed to Elizabeth's throne, Doll. I am committed to that, and my heart would not allow me otherwise." He uttered Queen Mary's name with a hushed reverence which Dorothy in her mood of heightened sensitivity could not fail to appreciate.

"Then so be it," she said. She could not condone his active support for a foreign monarch while the English one still lived, but she must respect him for his ideals, she felt. Just as she had allied herself to John, whatever the consequences, so Thomas had allied himself to the cause of the Scottish Queen – for better, for worse, for richer, for poorer ... "In *my* heart, I shall always be your friend," she told him.

"That I know, and I am glad of it," he said.

Now she knew for certain she must withhold her brother-in-law's views from John. Maybe that was her way of protecting Thomas – of protecting John too and being strong for once without him.

Soon it was William Tailbois' turn to be conducted around the garden and orchard, even though he had seen it several times before. The crystal waters of the fountain splashed softly into a mossy basin near the carved oak bench where they sat together afterwards, the old clerk who always dressed in black and his beautiful niece, with whom he delighted to talk of matters both great and deep. And he listened with especial interest to her revelations about Thomas.

"There are some who would call you a possessive woman, my dear," he told her, regarding her attempt to dissuade her brother-in-law.

"And you, Uncle?"

"I know you to be very loving – towards your own and those you make your own," he said, his large, friendly eyes twinkling at her. "You grow so attached to them that you reach out with both hands and try to hold on."

"Yet I cannot always do so. Is that what you wish to tell me?"

He surveyed her more quizzically, seeing the discouragement on her face. "You cannot keep conscience for those dear to you, Dorothy. Nor can you take personal responsibility for their actions."

"You are right, of course," she sighed. "If only I could see myself through your eyes!"

"You remind me so much of your mother," he smiled. "except that you have more spirit."

Dorothy's face brightened again, this mention of her mother, the sweetness of the garden, the softness of the summer evening lulling her into a mood of unexpected peace.

"Each day can be so uncertain," she suddenly said reluctantly. "I learnt that after she died."

"I learnt that long ago," he mused, "having lived under all these Tudor monarchs. Did you know I have changed my religion four times?"

They both laughed. "And may have to change it again, if the Queen of Scots comes south!"

"Hm," he replied. "How much of that is talk? I think it will be many years before she gains her heart's desire."

"I *hope* it will be many years."

"Then my earthly days will be over before I have to change again!"

There was a pause. Such thoughts made Dorothy feel sad again. Then she decided on a swift, firm change of subject, to the pleasures of delving into the past.

"There used to be a priory here at Uffington," she said. "Didn't you once live in a monastery?"

"Ah yes." He leaned back contentedly against the bench and off he went, about the wildness and beauty surrounding a remote abbey in Yorkshire, how his days were ruled by bells tolling inexorably for masses and matins and vespers, and stories, many stories, about the other monks, sometimes their misdemeanours, for some had cracked under the strain of solitude and penances, of fasts and silences, and the endless round of prayers. Then one day the commissioners came and closed the abbey. They closed all the abbeys.

"It caused much bitterness," he remembered. "Monks and nuns turned out, some into little more than beggars. I was fortunate; my family obtained for me a living."

"Did you feel bitter?" asked Dorothy.

"No, but I knew many who were. Your father, for instance."

"Why?" She fidgeted uneasily.

"He was very young, with all the impatience and energy of youth, and none of his later power. In Derbyshire, the monasteries were all laid waste to the ground and there was nothing he could do to prevent it." He sighed, then said more softly, "There was another reason."

"What?"

"His stepfather."

Dorothy moved closer, her face agog with interest. "John's uncle?" she whispered.

They both glanced furtively round. Then, faintly amused by

their childlike secrecy and satisfied that there was no-one else to share it, Uncle William continued, "Yes, Sir Richard Manners. The King granted him monastic lands in several counties. And that could only mean one thing – he took an active part in destroying the abbeys and was therefore suitably rewarded."

"Is that why my father was against him, against all the Manners family?" He nodded. "So now I know," she said.

"As I mentioned before, the abbeys aroused much bitterness. The Catholic men of the north rebelled."

"The Pilgrimage of Grace?"

"It was a disastrous failure. Wisely, your father did not take part."

"But they could rebel again," said Dorothy, suddenly alarmed. She was thinking once more of Thomas, of the Catholic stronghold of Lancashire where he belonged.

"Anything is possible, my dear," said her uncle.

He spoke the truth, she knew, but his words had not comforted her in the manner she had hoped. Yet she had found relief in voicing her thoughts to him and accepting his advice. Let Thomas and Margaret go their way and she go hers with John. He veered towards the English Queen, the Shrewsburys, and his path was easy for her to follow, especially enhanced by her friendship with Countess Gertrude. And curiously, Uncle William had healed that breach between herself and Margaret, for there would be no bitterness, she would make sure of that. They must accept their differences without reproach.

All animosity towards her sister had left her by the time they said farewell. John stood beside Dorothy in the courtyard as they watched their guests disappear through the gate. He looked down at his wife's face and teased her softly, "I see that this visit has set you aglow. I do believe I'm jealous of that look in your eyes!"

"My dearest love," she replied, turning to him. "I have benefited from their visit, for they have helped me to know myself much better."

But if her quarrel with Margaret was ended, it seemed that the name of Thomas could not stay out of Dorothy's mind for the rest of that year.

Gertrude gave birth to her eighth child, a son, and called him Thomas. Amid their happiness, Dorothy and John were to be his godparents – which meant that they were completely unprepared for the news which stunned them just before Christmas:

Gertrude and her baby had died, and the Earl already had plans to remarry.

ELEVEN

Dorothy mourned long the loss of Gertrude, but the weeks had mounted into months and on a dull November morning in 1568 she realized with some shock that the second anniversary of this noble lady's death would soon be upon them. What a tragedy that Gertrude had not lived to see her brother become Lord of Haddon. So soon afterwards, that had happened ... and later, Shrewsbury's second marriage had been highly approved of by Queen Elizabeth and though this had assured his new Countess of John's friendship, Dorothy felt far less euphoric.

Gazing into her mirror, Dorothy saw a white face looking back at her, "like a ghost", she pointed out to Joan.

"And that I will be one day," she mused. "And other faces will then reflect from this glass, the faces of my children and grandchildren ... and something of John and me will look out from them."

"Humph," grunted Joan. "What a way to talk when Master John will soon be home."

For an instant, delight leapt into Dorothy's face as she glanced at her dear maid and companion.

She had been resting late, for she was with child again and determined to take care this time. But she had arisen and dressed in a mood of unaccountable depression. An absurd mood, she told herself – but one which was not easily discarded.

My cup should be overflowing with bliss now, she thought sadly as Joan arranged her hair. Here she was in the situation she had dreamed about, living at Haddon with John and in the spring their baby would be born. Yet there were other events of great moment casting shadows over her happiness, events way beyond her control though nonetheless disturbing.

Mary Queen of Scots had now arrived in England – and under very different circumstances than those visualised by Thomas. She had fled from her own rebellious subjects only to find herself a prisoner of Elizabeth and was now held captive in Yorkshire.

In Yorkshire also were the Shrewsburys, whom John had been to visit. They were often in Derbyshire too, for the new Countess was none other than Lady Bess, the Manners' Chatsworth neighbour. Dorothy herself could smile now at the alarm she had suffered on Margaret's wedding day when she imagined either Bess or Lady Port allied to her father. Lord Shrewsbury, however, smiled little these days. He had been married to the lady for less than a year, yet already he knew who was master.

Dorothy was tugging impatiently at her gown when a startling thud suddenly arrested her attention.

"Twas a robin!" exclaimed Joan. "It flew straight into the window panes." She looked hesitantly at her mistress. "There will be a message soon," she said.

"Oh, you and your rustic superstitions!" scoffed Dorothy. But in her heart she was not so sure. What message could there possibly be? Even more ill tidings from the outside world?

"Maybe my husband will bring a message," she said more gently.

"What kind of message would you like?"

"Mm ... I know the kind I wouldn't like. News of another visit from the Countess!"

"Heaven forbid," agreed Joan, removing the peignoir from her mistress's shoulders.

Dorothy recalled the times when Bess had bounced into their lives. The peaceful atmosphere of their home was shattered then: orders were shouted, servants were harried and her own quiet efficiency seemed to vanish the more she tried to impress and please her guest.

She stopped, for it seemed hardly right to her that she should talk thus of a Countess with her maid. But such was the depth of her dislike! Besides, who was this woman but 'Bess of Hardwick' as the local folk still called her, the daughter of a minor country squire.

And so Dorothy went on, "In the company of his brisk wife, my Lord Earl appears mild and ineffectual. But we know better than to under-estimate him, don't we, Joan?"

"Aye, madam."

Dorothy wondered, aloud, whether the Countess did the same.

"I doubt it," Joan winked at her. "Her ladyship is too busy extracting obedience from him, poor man."

Dorothy sighed, "And yet I must be friends with her, you know, for John's sake and the Earl's."

Joan was tidying the room when Dorothy felt the baby move within her. She stifled a cry, she knew not whether of joy for her child or wretchedness for her sudden discomfort.

"'Tis George again," she joked breathlessly, seeing Joan's look of unease.

"George!" repeated the maid. Then, reassured, she began to laugh outright and after a minute Dorothy joined her.

"I'm serious!" she said at last. "George is a fine name for a son. What think you?"

The shining pleasure in Joan's eyes told its own tale. "Aye, sweet lady. A fine name. After your father, no doubt, and after the Earl."

Dorothy nodded quickly. "And it *will* be a son. You cannot know what that means to me."

"But to see you smile and laugh so much, I know what that means ..."

"Amen to that!" said a deep voice as the door opened.

Dorothy sprang up and whirled about towards its owner, almost flying at John as he entered. His arms opened out and caught her and then his mouth came down on hers.

"John, I have missed you so," she said.

"I know. It seems an age since I left you, sweetheart, though it was but two days ago."

He held her away from him a little as Joan curtsied and made her exit. Then he drew her to him again gladly.

She gazed questioningly into his face.

"What news do you bring from Lord Shrewsbury?"

"Nothing of great import. He hastens me back to you with his greeting."

She let out a sigh of unutterable relief and heartily embraced him.

"I cannot move very fast now, John," he teased her in a high-pitched voice. "Remember my condition!"

She blushed, then made a face at him as he laughingly released her. But her joy at his homecoming had chased away her dismal mood and she attached herself to him brightly for the rest of the day.

They lay in each other's arms that night, but afterwards they did not fall asleep. John stirred restlessly, unusually for him, while Dorothy, who had curled up to face him, remained very still as she watched him with increasing concern.

"John, what is it?" she whispered.

He held her close against him. He did not speak, but now lay staring upwards into the darkness.

"My dearest, what *is* it?" cried Dorothy more urgently, for suddenly his arm jerked violently.

"'Tis something trifling, Dorothy," he replied. "That's the annoying part of it. Lady Bess and her damned exasperating rumours ... I chide myself that I even took note –"

"Rumours? What about?"

"About the Queen the Scots. It is said she tried to escape and Quen Elizabeth intends to move her further south. God only knows what troubles that may bring to the Midlands."

Her indrawn breath was enough to tell him that she was frightened. He turned to her and kissed her. "I'm sorry to cause you distress, my love. I'll try to cease my worrying now. After all, there will always be rumours."

She understood that his dark mood was passing and in their togetherness he found comfort. But while John slept at last beside her, it was as though his fears had passed to her and in the morning, much to the disappointment of her maid, Dorothy's tenseness had returned.

However, in the coming weeks she was to reason this away to her servant with the words, "Forewarned was forearmed." That thud of the redbreast on the window took until December to oblige Joan's superstition, but then came the day when William Crossland arrived at Haddon.

Dorothy and John were alone together, relaxing in the great chamber and the news that "My Lord of Shrewsbury's man is here with a letter" seemed to her then an unwelcome intrusion into their lovely world.

"I'll warrant he is hungry," she cut in rather sharply to John's servant. "Pray see he is given food."

John shot her a look of bewilderment.

"Nay, Dorothy," he said gently, "it will not take long to see what the Earl has to say." Then turning to the servant, he ordered, "Send him to me immediately."

How fragile a thing was contentment! Dorothy instinctively placed her hands on her stomach as if to reassure the little entity inside. Her intuition had driven her to try and delay their knowledge of the Earl's message – intuition and a sudden strange feeling of apprehension. And why? For all she knew, the letter might be heartening. The silence seemed interminable until William Crossland knocked, then entered and John received the folded missive from him with a word of thanks.

He broke the seal and spread open the letter on the table. Dorothy watched him with bated breath – and saw John's right hand which had just smoothed out the paper, suddenly contract into a clenched fist.

"My God!" he shouted.

And then she was at his side staring down at the Gothic handwriting, aware that John's face was now strained too – and hardened. That beloved face which had been gazing at her so affectionately only a little while earlier.

"Dorothy, you were right," he said to her almost wonderingly. "You were right to be afraid."

With a further gesture of contempt, he scrunched the letter in his hand and flung it pell-mell across the table. "So much for dismissing those rumours," he added ruefully. "Not only is the Queen of Scots coming into the Midlands, but into the custody of new jailers. She is committed, until Elizabeth decrees otherwise – to the Earl and Countess of Shrewsbury!"

John and Dorothy learn that the captive queen is to be
placed in the Earl of Shrewsbury's custody

Francis Rolleston persuades Thomas to lead the plot to rescue
the captive Queen from Chatsworth

Shrewsbury and his wife, Bess of Hardwick, inform Dorothy and
John of the rescue plot

PART IV: 1570-71

'Nothing is certain in these days
But subject still to change all.
Therefore, tis best we change our ways,
That no mishap to us do fall.'

Thomas Whythorne

A conspiritorial meeting between John Hall, Francis Rolleston
and his son George

John Hall attempts to wrest Queen Mary's secret letter from
George Rolleston, to prevent betrayal of the plot

TWELVE

On a sunny afternoon in May, Dorothy was walking in the gardens of her home, enjoying the company of her baby son.

A sturdy, endearing child! she reflected with some amusement as she watched him. They had stopped yet again and the leading-strings which attached the boy to his mother were once more almost wrenched out of her hands. What was the use of leading-strings to aid him to walk, she wondered, when, if George wanted to have a rest, George merely stopped and sat down where he wished. Or if something caught his attention in the flower border he veered off without warning to poke an exploring finger into any flower within his reach.

Naturally, these frequent stops did tend to impede their progress around the gardens. But George seemed to be completely absorbed in his own contented little world.

It was now over a year since Dorothy had experienced the agonies of childbirth, those pain-dazed hours of labour when she had struggled to produce this determined little figure beside her. Her body had felt so weak after expelling the child, yet her clearest memories now were not so much of pain but of relief as she gazed at her women bustling around him. Relief, yes, and a deep feeling of gratitude for her safe delivery.

Dorothy walked on a little further with her son before he sat down again. This time she decided to join him, but as soon as she had settled herself comfortably on the lawn, George, making a joyful chuckling sound, stood up.

"Look!" she said, gently drawing his attention to the fact that his father was approaching them rapidly from the house.

George gurgled some excited, but unintelligible response immediately he saw John, and dropping on all fours, started crawling at top speed towards him, heedless of any obstacles such as leading-strings which might inhibit his movement. Dorothy let him go and laughed with pleasure as he threw himself against John's legs before being hoisted high up onto his shoulders.

"I cannot fault our son for forwardness," John grinned as he came up to Dorothy. "But we must return him to his nurse now."

"I suppose it is time we left for Chatsworth," said Dorothy.

"I fear so. Tis only courtesy to visit our kinsman when he is living so near. It is not as though my Lord Earl can visit us nowadays."

"No," she sighed as they entered the house. "How he must miss calling on his friends!"

"Especially his friends at Court."

Dorothy felt sorry for the Earl. He had once gone often to Court and been held in the highest favour. As a sign of that favour, he had been entrusted with the task of guarding the Queen of Scots. But now he was virtually a prisoner himself, moving about with his "charge" as he termed her from one Midland home to another. First to Tutbury Castle, then Wingfield Manor, back to Tutbury again and now, Chatsworth.

She was glad to find that Shrewsbury received them alone in his apartments there.

"Lady Bess is with the Queen," he apologized with his usual air of harassment these days. "No doubt you will see her anon."

Dorothy smiled and was content in leave the two men to their conversation. Any talk of ships and lead mining did not hold her interest at the best of times, even more so when here she was in the very same building as the famous Queen of Scots! She moved across to the window, hoping that her smile had not seemed too much like a smirk when the Earl had mentioned seeing the Countess anon. She knew she would much rather catch a discreet glimpse of the romantic royal captive.

Scots. To Dorothy, the word had once sounded like a hiss, but that was before she had met Queen Mary.

Almost a year ago now, she thought, but it was a meeting she would always remember. Dorothy and John had gone to see the Shrewsburys at Wingfield Manor and the Queen of Scots, though clearly very ill, had shown both warmth and interest in young George.

"Alas, I have lost my own child," she had confided to Dorothy. And the look of sadness on her lovely face had made a deep impression on the Lady of Haddon.

Well may John tease her that she had succumbed to the noted charm of the Scottish Queen. But there was more to it than that. What Dorothy felt was the sympathy of one young mother for another – another who had been separated from her own baby. Womanly compassion, something that John could not fully understand, but his wife had found an unexpected affinity with this Queen. They were much of an age, and Dorothy knew that whatever sufferings had afflicted Mary Queen of Scots, the greatest punishment of all was the enforced separation from her son.

"Well, my dear," said the voice of Shrewsbury at her side, "it is some time since you saw my royal charge. There she is!"

Dorothy followed the direction of his finger towards a group of figures walking in the grounds below.

"Oh!" she said involuntarily. What she meant was, "Oh, the indignity!" Did the tall and beautiful woman in the centre of the group really need so many guards?"

Dorothy had controlled her words, but somehow Shrewsbury grasped her line of thought. "Yes, I am afraid they are necessary," he explained. "There have been too many plots to rescue her."

"And so far they have failed."

"So far," he repeated.

They turned away from the window, and it was only then that Dorothy noticed John studying some papers which the Earl had given him, studying them with a fixed sombre intensity on his face. She was sure that he hadn't looked up once from those papers when the Queen of Scots passed by. No, no-one could accuse John of succumbing to her charm!

No-one could accuse the Countess either, thought Dorothy, as Bess suddenly stormed into the room.

"Ah," nodded Shrewsbury anxiously. "As you see, my lady, we have visitors."

"Yes," Bess checked herself, and with a tone of icy control exchanged the customary formalities with Dorothy and John.

"Your precious Queen has gone to her bower," she sharply informed her husband.

"Poor lady," mumbled Shrewsbury.

"Poor lady, huh!" snapped Bess.

Poor Shrewsbury, more likely! Dorothy moved very close to John and they glanced briefly at each other, a look of understanding which sympathised with the Earl. Was there ever a time, Dorothy wondered, when Bess was young and sweet-natured and spoke without meaning to wound? Or was she born hard?

"Queen Mary finds my wife's house much to her liking," said Shrewsbury, addressing no-one in particular.

"Her bower?" asked Dorothy quietly.

"Her little garden," he replied. "Come, my dear." He gently conducted Dorothy to another window. "See those trees over there?" She nodded. "Behind there is a moat and in the centre is a tower with a garden on its roof."

"A flat roof?" she enquired.

"That's right. To reach the tower, you have to cross over a little stone bridge."

"It must be very beautiful," she said.

"It *is*," Bess affirmed.

Dorothy had been aware of the Countess's eagle eyes upon them, but their praise of her beloved Chatsworth had obviously softened Bess a little.

She excused herself from their presence and no sooner had she left the room than the atmosphere relaxed immediately.

"I am glad you were here," observed Shrewsbury.

"Why?" asked John, amused.

"Well, I fear she came to reprove me once more for my laxity. She says I reward too many of my friends with glimpses of my charge."

"And do you, my lord?"

"Of course. She is right, you know. Bess is *always* right," sighed the Earl wearily.

"Then maybe you should heed her words," suggested John.

"Aye. Maybe I will."

But Shrewsbury's eyes twinkled at Dorothy, as if conveying to her his reluctance to obey Bess.

She smiled back in acknowledgement. If the Queen of Scots must be held captive, at least, Dorothy knew, she could not have a kindlier jailer than my Lord of Shrewsbury.

A few days later, a group of horsemen followed the homeward journey of Dorothy and John, from Chatsworth towards Haddon.

"To meet the Queen of Scotland! It was the greatest honour," remarked Thomas Stanley to his brother.

"I can see she clearly charmed you."

"And you, Ned."

Sir Edward Stanley gave a sudden, harsh laugh. "As for the Great Earl, he is not so great beside his new Countess."

"Strange," mused Thomas, "how some women get their way by domineering and others by clinging femininity."

"Give me clinging femininity every time!" quipped Edward Stanley.

"You're thoughtful," said Thomas to his two older companions.

Sir Thomas Gerard and Francis Rolleston appeared to regard him shrewdly.

"We have good reason to be," said Rolleston, "ever since the bull."

"The bull?"

"Papal bull." He made the sign of the cross. "My son tells me that a Londoner nailed it to the Bishop's palace."

"They arrested him, poor wretch," observed Gerard.

"Who, the Londoner?" cried Edward Stanley. "The devil they did!"

"But what did the bull say exactly?" asked Thomas.

"Elizabeth is excommunicated. And what's more ..." Rolleston hesitated for a moment, waiting for Edward Stanley's high, clear whoop of delight to subside. "And what's more, her Catholic subjects are no longer bound to obey her."

"*I* am a Catholic!" shouted Edward Stanley, exultant.

"I too," said Gerard firmly, "and I am tired of pretending to be a Protestant. Why, under the late Catholic Queen, my own family and my wife's, the Ports of Etwall, prospered."

"There was a time when I was loyal to Elizabeth," recalled Thomas.

His brother sneered, "I thought you were all for Mary Stuart."

"I am, but …"

"But what?"

"She is a prisoner," retorted Thomas with a note of finality in his voice.

Edward Stanley gave a snort of disgust, which Thomas chose to ignore.

"I was a prisoner also," Gerard grumbled.

"I am sorry for you," said Thomas. "Three years is a long time to suffer for your faith."

"And how I have suffered under Elizabeth! Heavy fines, imprisonment in the Tower. Even now I attend her church only to save my fortune from wasting away."

They rode on in sullen and pensive silence.

"It would be best to talk of other matters now we are nearing Haddon," Thomas reminded them. "You know well my brother-in-law's opinions."

The limestone walls of Haddon came strikingly into view, and Edward Stanley licked his lips as if some tasty dish had been set before him.

"But for Shrewsbury and his kin," he mused, reining in his horse, "this fair sight could have been mine now."

"Have done, Ned! That's all in the past."

"Yes, Tom, all in the past. But I tell you this, he's still no friend of mine."

In the great chamber at Haddon that evening, John Manners surveyed his guests, amid joining in the card games and surface pleasantries. He could look back now on a day he had not wanted to face, a day which he knew would bring problems. And here they were, four of them, in the shape of his principal guests. Avowed Papists, all of them, except perhaps Thomas – and he had long had his misgivings about Thomas.

His eyes drifted across to the corner of the room where Dorothy and Thomas were playing 'tables'. Heads bent closely together, they seemed to be in their own enclosed world, talking and laughing in their private, animated way. So his wife and her brother-in-law found pleasure in each other's company. He had never begrudged them that, but John did not need to eavesdrop on them to know what they were prattling so excitedly about. The Queen of Scots – again!

He yawned, then smiled across at them, a bland smile to hide the anxiety he felt for both. Just lately, there were times when Dorothy seemed to be looking at him without seeing him. It was all very well for wealthy romantics like Thomas to be prompted by curiosity into visiting Lord Shrewsbury's charge, but he did not welcome their influence on his young wife.

Dorothy! He gazed at her now with tender exasperation. So spirited at times, so impulsive, yet her deep and unquestioning devotion to him he had always thought unshakable. Until recently. He would have a gentle word in her ear, he decided, as he concentrated once more on his game. Yes, that would bring them back together again. And soon. Tomorrow. No-one, he was determined, *no-one* would embroil his Dorothy in any murky intrigues surrounding Mary Queen of Scots!

Little by little, as the hours ebbed slowly away into the next day, John's preoccupation with these thoughts increased. He could not bring himself to broach the matter while his guests were still under his roof. And so he waited, he bided his time until they had all departed. It was late afternoon by then. Late afternoon, and how long had been his brooding! A chill wind seemed to be blowing towards Haddon, straight out of the on-rushing future, and suddenly he wanted to press it back, nay, beat it off with all his might. For if any mishap befell Dorothy, any scandal concerning the Queen of Scots ... His thoughts had swept away all his accustomed calm, leaving behind in their wake a desperate, unfamiliar mood of fear, a mood so dangerous that it could flame like dry tinder. And it was ready to receive its spark.

The nursery door was wide open and peals of laughter coming out as John sought the presence of his wife. He paused for a moment at the top of the stairs, not wanting to disturb their game. There was a happy glow about the two figures he could see, a touching innocence, and he was, after all, on the outside looking in.

The baby, propped on a pile of cushions on the floor, chortled merrily every time his mother peered out at him from behind the high back of the settle. In between times, when she was hiding, his face was a picture of shining anticipation, waiting for her to re-appear.

"Boh!" Sometimes she looked out at him from above the settle, sometimes from one side and then the other. "We shall be going away soon," said Dorothy, crouching behind the settle once more. "Away!" Her head popped up again, and George collapsed into a fresh bout of convulsive laughter.

She rushed to his side, endeavouring at last to calm him, which she did in a soothing voice. "Yes, we are going away, my son, a long, long way from here. All the way to Wilton, to see Lord Pembroke and his wife." The baby gurgled as she picked him up. "They are very grand, those people," she said.

She turned to sit in the rocking chair, with George now quiet on her lap. "And so we are going together, not like the Queen of Scotland, poor, sad lady, who cannot have her baby with her ..."

At that, John looked briefly and vehemently up to the ceiling and suddenly burst into the room. He noticed her stiffen and the glow fade from her face.

"W-why do you look so grim?" she stuttered. "Has something happened?"

George wriggled on her lap, and not without displeasure as she clutched him tightly to her.

John still kept his distance. "We cannot go on like this," he said bluntly.

"What do you mean, John? I don't understand."

And then he flared at her, "Scots, Scots! All you talk about is Mary Queen of Scots! Is it not bad enough that we live within her shadow? I can accept that, Dorothy, I can accept many things. But these constant reminders, you drive me beyond the edge of endurance."

Dorothy winced at his fury. It had been part of their loving that from time to time he should pretend to be angry with her, but this, they both knew, was no pretence.

"And now you talk of her to our son," he thundered on, "talking unwisely to him of some sad illusion inside your romantic head. Do you no longer care for him, let alone for me?"

He stopped, giving her the chance to justify herself, to fling back her own wrath at him as he expected her to. But instead she seemed to droop like a spent flower. Straying auburn curls from the loose folds of her hair mingled with the soft, fair curls of the child as she buried her face against him.

"I can only think," she whispered, "that you did not mean what you said."

She sniffed, then George, as if sensing that he was one of the subjects of discussion, suddenly began to wail, a great abundance of tears for his sorrow. There was no need for her to cry, for he was doing so for both of them. She began to rock him to and fro.

"Sweetheart," said John more gently.

No response.

"Sweetheart!"

Still no response. His voice then rose to a tone of urgent pleading. "Can't you see that in my clumsy way I'm trying to protect you? Don't you know it's perilous to express your sympathies too openly?"

She looked at him with dilated eyes.

"Am I so unwise," she asked, "because I feel pity for a captive who suffers in exile?"

"She is no ordinary captive."

"No, she could be England's next Queen."

"Then reserve your friendship for her until that day," he advised. "You do not seem to realize that if your feelings for the prisoner were too well-known, you could so easily be drawn into intrigues around her. Dorothy, people have died for their sympathy to her cause!"

"I do not see," she went on, "why her present position, the circumstances of her life, could not be improved. It need not injure Elizabeth."

"God's death!" he exploded again. "Are you a fool, Dorothy? She is imprisoned for her own safety, for the safety of the realm."

"Yes, you have made that perfectly clear," she said, still in control of herself.

With her gentle comforting, the baby at last drained himself dry of tears, but continued to regard his father mournfully.

John came and knelt beside them. "As for you, my heart's life," he said, lightly caressing her face, "your safety is my concern."

She kissed his hand, and then his other arm stole across the front of the chair, so that both his wife and child were within close touch of it, symbolically protected.

"Forgive me," he went on, "for hurting you so. I feared for you, Dorothy. I fear still for others, Thomas and the Earl included."

"These are days of growing tension, John, and tempers can run so high."

"How right you are! And yet you do not know how right."

"What should I know?"

He seated himself on the settle. "Well, the Pope has washed his hands of Queen Elizabeth – and released all her Catholic subjects from their duties of allegiance to her."

Dorothy gasped at the news. "Why didn't Thomas tell me this?"

"Maybe he doesn't know yet. But I have my contacts at Court."

"Oh, John," she cried impulsively, "how glad I am that we are not Thomas or Lord Shrewsbury. It is so much better to be us."

"Right again!" he grinned. "I am not sure about Thomas, but discontent is rife amongst his Papist friends. All they need is a Catholic Queen to receive their full-sworn loyalty. And here she is, in our very midst!"

"Poor Shrewsbury. I do not envy him his charge."

"But we owe him our support, Dorothy, now more so than ever." John came to her side once more. "Remember what he did for us."

"How could I ever forget?" They both smiled.

"Promise me, then, sweetheart, you will keep well away from

any intrigues and keep private your feelings about the Queen of Scots."

"I promise," she told him firmly. "Romantic I may be, and liable to make mistakes. But you are my whole life, you and the babe ..."

She looked down at their offspring, but George had long since lost interest in the proceedings and now slept peacefully in her arms.

The sparkle returned to her eyes. "Whatever happened to your romance, John?"

"'Tis kept exclusively for you!" His own eyes were still blazing blue, but blazing now with joy instead of anger.

He took the baby from her arms and laid him carefully in his cradle. George roused a little, opening his eyes as the covers descended over him. But then sleep claimed him back once more, and there was no movement, only the sound of quiet breathing.

Here, it seemed, in this one little haven of Haddon Hall that love had re-asserted its strength in the midst of turmoil and misunderstanding. And John wanted to hold on to this precious gift as he had never done so before. All the weeks he had felt unable to reach Dorothy, they had now melted away, and her mind had turned back to meet his. She had followed him across the room to the cradle, and his arms were around her, and their togetherness was a light in life's gathering storm.

How good that the sun was still shining and the summer was not far off.

"Thank God," John murmured with relief, "that we are leaving restless Derbyshire behind, for the summer months at least."

THIRTEEN

In Wiltshire, the Peak District did indeed seem far away. There had been visits to Salisbury, with its cathedral spire soaring gracefully heavenwards, and to lonely and desolate Stonehenge.

What manner of monument was this? thought Dorothy. Wrought by men from the dim and distant past? Yet it too had filled her with a sense of awe and mystery, those massive stones stirring visions of home – of Harthill and Stanton Moors with their stone circles, and Arbor Low, perched high amid wild and windswept land.

Yes, her mind still wandered back to Derbyshire. There had been times when she feared her relationship with John had reached its own peak and the fire was beginning to burn low. But now, though neither of them ever mentioned their quarrel, she knew that his need for her had deepened and they could share with each other freely again all their hopes and their concerns.

How many summers had passed since she met John! That summer at Wingfield Manor when she had helped little Katherine Talbot with her embroidery. Katherine was now the Countess of Pembroke, their hostess at Wilton House. She had been married to a man much older than herself and as yet there were no children. Her husband was a kindly and generous host. He held high offices under Queen Elizabeth and spent much of the year at Court, but he was glad to retire to his country retreat for his first summer there as Earl. Not that Wilton was a secluded place. Far from it! It seemed that he and his Countess had brought some of the gaiety of Court life with them.

"I am for the time a country man and I go hunting with my lord every day," wrote John in his letter to the Earl of Rutland.

Dorothy teased him when she read this, "I wonder that you have time for writing letters – hunting often till twilight and then dancing till close on midnight!"

He met her gaze with shining eyes.

"I see that you too find life at Wilton agreeable."

"Whatever gave you that idea?" she smiled with a hint of mischief.

"Your appetite has improved."

"I'm feeling remarkably well nowadays," she admitted. "I came here thinking of this place as a refuge, a convenient means of escape."

"And do you find it more than that? If so, then I am glad."

"It is an enchanting place," said Dorothy. "A whole new world of enjoyment."

The weeks of June and early July were enlivened with rumours that Queen Elizabeth might visit Wilton during the course of her summer progress. But then news came that she had gone into Buckinghamshire instead and so Katherine announced to Dorothy one day, "My lord has given me leave to go to Derbyshire, for we hear my father is ailing."

"He lives under considerable strain," sympathized Dorothy.

"He lives on the edge of a precipice!" cried her friend.

She nodded in reply, judging best to say no more of Lord Shrewsbury's bitter situation, which was fully understood by them both.

Katherine, however, confided, "I like well enough my lady stepmother, but I know that when Lady Gertrude died, the happiest part of my father went with her."

Dorothy moved towards her, sensing her distress. "God keep you on your journey to him, and I pray he will soon recover."

Katherine thanked her and then hugged her with great affection, saying, "Another friend of yours will bide with you until I return."

"Lady Maud?"

"Who else? We Derbyshire folk must stick together!"

Dorothy smiled at her, though these fresh reminders of her native county had brought on a mood of resignation.

Dear God, the whole county is living on the edge of a precipice! she thought. She hoped with a desperate hope that no-one would stray too near the brink. Since her arrival at Wilton, Dorothy had learnt that merely to talk of Queen Elizabeth being succeeded by another was treason. And how often had she talked of it, with Thomas, with Margaret, even with John?

But John had given her very short shrift when she did so and now once again he was the rock in her life. Nothing was certain to her apart from that, apart from her faith. If ever Queen Mary's supporters rallied enough forces to her cause and won the English throne for her, what would become of her jailer? What would become of him if she escaped? The consequences were unthinkable, for of course he would be held responsible.

Poor Shrewsbury, thought Dorothy yet again. His task is impossible.

Soon after Katherine's departure, Sir Francis and Lady Maud Hastings rode beneath the fine Tudor archway of Wilton House and dismounted in its paved courtyard.

Dorothy's heart lifted again when she saw Maud's bright face and the warm smile of her husband.

"You have brought good weather with you," she said, embracing her stepmother.

"In this part of England, the climate always seems good to me," Maud replied, turning brilliant eyes towards her spouse.

"And are you happy then?" whispered Dorothy in conspiratorial tones.

"*Very* happy."

Sir Francis kissed his wife with a great kindness and realizing that his presence seemed somewhat superfluous, he respectfully took his leave of the two ladies to attend to "sundry other matters".

"Dorothy, you have cut yourself!" cried Maud, noticing her confidante's left hand.

"Tis naught," Dorothy reassured her. "The needle pricked into my hand instead of my embroidery yesterday, I'm afraid. My thoughts were away elsewhere."

"There, that will cure it."

And to Dorothy's amazement, Maud stroked the very slight wound with the finger which held her wedding ring.

"My lady, what magical power is this?" she asked, pretending to frown.

"Tis not what you think," said Maud. "Tis not – witchcraft. Call it custom, call it superstition if you will, but in Somerset, my adopted county, they believe that the ring-finger will heal any sore or wound which is stroked or rubbed by it."

"That's all right then!" teased Dorothy, slipping her arm through Maud's as they tripped lightly into the house.

"In Somerset ..." Maud went on, and so continued during the next few days with such an obvious love for her new surroundings that Dorothy forgot her gloomy thoughts and fended off that nightmare feeling that most of life was balanced on dangerous uncertainties. In her very real need to do so, no company could have been better for her than the supremely happy Maud.

August came in with warm, still days and Katherine returned to them, quietly satisfied with her worthwhile visit to her father.

She began recounting this to them in detail, laughing as she fanned herself vigorously that the air seemed so heavy here compared with Derbyshire's cool breezes.

As she continued, the name of a Papist called John Hall was mentioned.

"John Hall?" Maud suddenly interrupted her. "Yes, I have heard of him – through my stepsister, Lady Gerard."

"He was a servant of my lord father's," Katherine explained, "and retains good standing in his household."

"Does he?" asked Maud, surprised.

"Why yes. I even travelled with him from the home of one Derbyshire friend to another. Is there some reason why you don't like him?"

"Nay, I've never met the man. I merely know that my stepsister has little enthusiasm for him."

Katherine gave a shrug, as if to say that Lady Gerard was entitled to her opinion and then their conversation drifted on. Casually, Dorothy mulled over her companions' former words and in her mind some names began forming a Catholic chain – John Hall, Lady Gerard, Sir Thomas Gerard – then she realized that the latter was with Sir Thomas and Sir Edward Stanley the last time she saw him.

She caught her breath at this particular link, for, odd though it seemed to her, Maud's light remarks about John Hall had disquieted her. And the feeling somehow seemed worse because she knew there was discontent amongst Thomas's Papist friends – friends for whom Hall could be a direct contact with the house where their Queen was held.

Dorothy tried to dismiss the name-chain as a figment of her imagination. But then again, she thought, it may be real. Unwittingly she stroked her brow with the ring-finger of her left hand, stopped and then pondered – if the men in this chain should now join together, what fresh intrigues could threaten Lord Shrewsbury?

As the following day dawned in Derbyshire, a man stood alone on the high moors above Chatsworth. He was waiting, listening to the throb of hoof beats growing nearer through the morning mist. Eventually, two riders emerged in front of him.

"Master Hall, Master Rolleston," acknowledged the man as John Hall and Francis Rolleston reined in their horses. "And what is your business with me?"

"We wish to effect the Queen's rescue," Hall replied.

"If Her Majesty will allow us to make plans," added Rolleston.

John Beaton, master of the Scottish Queen's household, showed interest if not excitement. "Are there other gentlemen to aid you?"

"Sir Thomas Gerard, Sir Edward Stanley," said Hall, "and if we can persuade him, Sir Thomas Stanley also."

"Derby's sons?" The Scotsman looked impressed.

"Aye, if Sir Thomas Stanley is with us, then all will be set fair," put in Rolleston. "As Governor of the Isle of Man he could sail Her Majesty to safety there and then wherever she likes best – Scotland, France ..."

"It will be our responsibility to convey her from here to the Lancashire coast," explained his companion.

"And how do you propose to free her from Chatsworth?"

"That we have not yet decided."

"But surely Chatsworth is less secure than most of her prisons," suggested Rolleston. "If only Her Majesty could escape to the height of these moors, we would meet her there with horses and the rescue be swiftly accomplished."

Beaton asked, "When do you envisage her resuce?"

"By night?"

The Scotsman looked doubtful.

"Well, day then," said Rolleston, a trifle exasperated as Hall also shrugged his shoulders.

"I can tell you neither yea or nay," said Beaton, "until I have consulted with Queen Mary herself. Do you both meet me here this evening and I will bring you her reply."

Darkness was already descending by the time the three men met again. Hall and Rolleston regarded John Beaton with earnest eyes, but there was no answering light from the holes of shadow upon his face.

"Her Majesty Queen Mary thanks you most graciously for your efforts on her behalf," he began in a low voice. "But she bids me tell you that she wishes no men to go about freeing her unless they are absolutely certain they will succeed."

The Derbyshire men looked downcast at him. During the hours of daylight, they had both indulged in hopes of future glory, vague dreams of changing the course of English history through their valiant deeds. Now, within an instant, those hopes had apparently been dashed.

"However," continued Beaton in a brighter tone, "Her Majesty has asked me to deliver to you this cipher." He handed this to Rolleston. "Using this, you may write to assure her of your good faith towards her and outline more clearly how her escape can be achieved."

"We will bring our reply to you here in ten days," said Rolleston determinedly.

"Until the 13th then, my friend," smiled Beaton. "God speed you with your plans."

Three days later, Rolleston arrived at Lathom House, the home of the Earl of Derby.

Thomas Stanley received him warmly in his apartments in the Eagle Tower.

"I know why you have come," he said.

"Sir Thomas Gerard has told you of our plans?"

"He has."

"Are you with us in this matter?"

"You can trust me not to betray your secret."

"But we need more from you, Sir Thomas, much more," Rolleston went on. "You are our key to success or failure. If by your good offices Queen Mary could reach the Isle of Man ..."

Thomas poured wine into two goblets and offered him one, glancing pensively at him as he did so.

"So this plot is merely to help her escape? There are no plans to proclaim her as Queen of England?"

"None that I know of," replied Rolleston, "though I dare say many people would welcome her!"

Thomas grinned in his engaging way, then took a few careful sips from his cup. He could not quite find the best words to express his own principles in the light of the other man's burning fanaticism. Their heartfelt sympathy for the Queen of Scots was something they had in common. She was a beautiful woman, a queen, an undeserving prisoner. Yet still his resolution wavered to become a party to this plot. How could he have known when he first showed loyalty to her cause that she would soon afterwards lose her Scottish throne and become a closely-guarded captive in England.

"Maybe this will help you to decide," said Rolleston, producing the cipher. "Queen Mary knows you. You have written to her before."

"That is true."

"Then I beg you to do so again, my friend. The most important letter of your life!"

They began to discuss practicalities – how she could leave Chatsworth by night and flee to the high moors, from where a strong party of horsemen, her own supporters, would bring her into Lancashire – and how, after that, Thomas himself could conduct her safely out of England.

The problem of how to get her out of Chatsworth came nearer to a solution. Beaton had said that she and her servants were locked in their rooms at night, but apparently Shrewsbury was so lax that there were no guards beneath her windows. At the mention of windows, a bell suddenly rang in Thomas's mind, for he knew someone else who had escaped from a Derbyshire house by night. She too was a young and auburn-haired beauty and she had succeeded by means of her chamber window!

"I will think on it," declared Thomas at last. "Pray leave the cipher with me."

For the first time, Rolleston had cause to smile. "Queen Mary will be convinced. She will give her blessing to our plans, but only you, Sir Thomas, can convince her."

He turned to make towards the door, but paused before he opened it. "One final thing, Sir Thomas."

"Yes?"

"I would recommend to you one of our number, a Derbyshire gentleman by the name of Hall. Should you be so good as to draft a letter, please send for him and he will transcribe it into coded form. Sir Thomas Gerard will sign it with you."

When Rolleston had left him, Thomas more than kept his promise to think on the matter. "Thought, thought!" he could almost hear his brother reviling him. "Too much thought, too much conscience!" He felt glad somehow that Ned was away in the north courting a Mistress Strickland. If he had been here, Ned would not have hesitated to commit himself to this plot. A man of action, that was he, and Thomas would have suffered unending derision.

Best leave Ned to his wenching, he decided, but I'll not deprive him of his chance to partake in this plot. If I endorse a letter, so will he, even if I have to sign it for him!

He smiled as he thought that. For once Ned would be pleased with him. And Margaret? Perhaps it was well too that she and their son were not here. They had stayed behind at Tong Castle. But he could trust her. Dear, comforting wife with her down-to-earth acceptance of whatever God sent her! No, there would be no problems with Margaret, whichever path Thomas chose.

There was another to consider too. What would his father say? If anything, Lord Derby had now changed course towards the Protestant Church of England, even having some Catholic recusants tried at Lathom. And to his sons' astonishment he had given Elizabeth a timely warning about the northern Catholics' rebellion last year. Thomas believed his noble father would neither help nor hinder the plot. Maybe in his old age he remembered more and more that without the Stanleys, the Tudors would never have gained the English throne at all. It was still less than a hundred years since the 1st Earl of Derby, Thomas's ancestor, had placed the crown on King Henry VII's head after their victory on Bosworth Field.

Thomas closed his eyes and rocked his chair to and fro. One day there could be honours anew for the Stanleys with this

Catholic Queen on the throne. But first she had to escape …

Suddenly his mind travelled back four summers to a lovingly tended garden in Lincolnshire and a girl full of charm and sisterly concern. *"We are two of a kind, you and I,"* he had said to Dorothy. *"There are times in our lives when we feel compelled to reach out for what we want, no matter what troubles we may have to face."* He had felt bold and reckless then, like his brother, but now that the opportunity had presented itself to reach out for what he wanted, he was unsure that he was prepared to face troubles. He was too fond of the good things of life – and of life itself, if truth be known.

Adventurous, romantic, Dorothy had called him with sincerity. Romantic he did not doubt. But adventurous? Compared with Ned, no! He smiled again. How Dorothy had changed to favour the Queen of Scots! Yet he did not have the heart to implicate her in any intrigue. Or did he? No-one else could advise him on nocturnal escapes through windows, or had such ready access to the Shrewsbury menage.

He must have fallen into a light doze, for although he was aware of being at ease in his chair, he also seemed to hear the piercing cries of seagulls and the roar of waves crashing against a rocky islet. The scene unfolding before him was so vivid that he recognized it immediately. He was back on the island again, at Peel, and the two boys within the scene were Ned and himself at play.

Close in age, they had been through many escapades together. As the youngest of a large family, Ned had been spoilt and petted by his sisters. Yet how often had he been the instigator of their boyish adventures and how often had Thomas either covered up for him or taken the blame instead! Thomas's good looks, his vitality and charming manners had proved invaluable to him on those occasions and in fact, throughout his life. He had the ability to draw men to him – women also, and now others were pressing him to lead this plot.

There was one childhood incident in particular which stood out in Thomas's memory. His brother was prone to oddly distracted moods and was noticeable by his absence at the most inconvenient times. At Peel, Ned could always be found in the same place – inside the cathedral staring as if bewitched into the blackness of a hole which led down to the prison cell beneath the bishop's chapel.

If anyone asked him what he was doing, he would start guiltily at first, then relax and grin, "Oh, just listening to the sea."

This became a kind of game between the two boys, until the day it took on a more sinister, though predictable turn. After the customary words, Ned grinned extra wickedly, laughed wildly for a moment and suddenly lurched through that entrance to the darkness.

Thomas's attempts to call him back were greeted by the most stinging abuse.

"Come down and get me! You coward, coward!"

Those latter words echoed hauntingly around the cathedral, provoking Thomas to a frenzy he had not known he possessed. A coward he certainly was not, and to prove it he stormed down that hole after his brother.

It was the most fearsome place he had ever encountered. The steep, narrow, slimy stairs he all but fell down and below him, the angry sea rose in a continuous roar as it lashed through the hollows of the rocky cavern. He was afraid it would break in on them at any moment and sweep them away to a terrifying end. He wanted to scream and scream, disturbing the eternal rest of those long buried in the vaults of the dead above them. But he dared not show his feelings in front of Ned and dared not leave until his brother was ready. Thomas was only nine years old at the time, but even now in his maturity he sometimes still heard that defiant and deafening sea.

No such horrors for Ned though! He had been fascinated by this cell to the point of obsession and before Thomas was allowed to leave, he coolly instructed him, "Count the pillars before you flee! Count the pillars or you will one day here in prison be!"

Ned praised himself for his witty chanting, but Thomas hurriedly counted the pillars, remembering this local superstition. There were thirteen in all, holding up the chapel above. After that, he began to feel less frightened, as if some dreadful threat had been lifted from him. And with true generosity he was soon back on amiable terms with this rascal brother of his, who seemed capable of showing his affection for Thomas only by taunting him.

In the chapel above, however, they met their older brother, Henry. He was obviously waiting for them and since he no longer had to wait, he unleashed his own torrent of abusive words at them, forbidding them ever to go down that hell-hole again. As usual, Thomas took most of the blame. As usual he called on all the charm at his disposal to make light of the situation and as usual, Henry melted under its influence while Ned remained impervious.

Caught in the middle! That was the story of Thomas's life. Sometimes appeasing his older brother, then striving to please the younger. But fate had always thrown in his lot with Edward rather than Henry.

And now he felt trapped in the conflict between two Queens, but still his life was more bound up with Ned, who favoured Catholic Mary, than it was with Henry, who supported Elizabeth.

He started up suddenly and stretching, staggered as if impelled towards the window. The sounds of seagulls and waves inside his head would not leave him alone, though in reality only a small flock of sparrows chirped happily nearby and there was no watery sound other than the gentle lapping of the moat against Lathom's outer wall.

Thomas had his own strong defences against any derision which Henry might hurl at him. But where Ned was concerned, he knew already that his will was weakening. Imagine the insults if he refused to enter the darkness of this plot and Ned found out!

There was, besides that, another matter to take into account –

Only one man, a very powerful man, had ever deliberately humiliated his younger brother. And Ned had neither forgotten, nor forgiven. Thomas himself had not forgotten, but if he had forgiven, why did it still plague him that he had done nothing to help Ned in that spring of 1563? There was little he could have done, he supposed, being tucked far away on the island. Thanks to the Great Earl, Dorothy was already the wife of another before Thomas was told. Ah well, let it be, he had thought then. Now he wished with all his heart that he had done something to help Ned.

But now he could! Of course, here was his chance at last! His enthusiasm for Mary Queen of Scots had ebbed since her imprisonment. Suddenly it was pouring through him again in full spate. Thomas charged across his chamber, sat down at the table and immediately began to write.

The letter formed before him, no mild, half-hearted supplication, but a proud and passionate appeal to his Sovereign Lady to give sanction to her rescue. He was ready to die in her cause. Why, if she did not desire to leave England but fight instead for the throne, he and Sir Thomas Gerard could raise 12,000 armed men from Lancashire alone, not to mention the 6,000 others from Catholic friends in Derbyshire. And the Pope would send help. He would provide soldiers from abroad. The Catholics of Europe regarded Mary, not the Protestant Elizabeth, as the rightful Queen of England. Welcome the day when she would restore the true faith to its former glory!

Should this plot succeed, how great would be Shrewsbury's downfall, he thought with an air of satisfaction.

And all the while Thomas was writing to Mary, the waves were roaring and crashing about his ears and his whole spirit cried out, "Revenge! Revenge on Lord Shrewsbury for humiliating my brother!"

FOURTEEN

On the day when Thomas wrote his letter, Dorothy was in a mood of despondency. She had now firmly convinced herself that something untoward was brewing up near her home and though she had tried hard to stave off her agitation by immersing herself as before in the endless social round at Wilton, she had to admit that life there was no longer an effective distraction for her.

Whenever she was alone with her thoughts, the dam she had built to block out her fears burst and left her unsure of herself. For half of her now felt tempted to go back to Derbyshire earlier than she and John had planned and try to find out what might be happening there first hand. She had contemplated writing to Thomas on the matter, but did not know his exact whereabouts. Perhaps that was just as well! pointed out her more rational thoughts. And if she did go home soon, goodness knows what harebrained schemes she might plunge into ...

Pacing their apartments, Dorothy only vaguely heard the hunting party's return and somehow her habit of going to greet John caught no immediate spark in her mind this time.

She glanced remotely towards the doors and was suddenly startled back to consciousness when she realized that she had left it partly open. And what was more, the door was moving further open! From where she stood, rigid, it completely hid whoever was coming in.

A tiny hand appeared low, round the rim of the door, followed by a happy, trusting little face. Then all of George toddled into the room, almost choking with laughter.

With a cry of sudden joy, she swooped down to hold him, but George playfully eluded her and scampered back through the doorway. He then peered round at her again as if to say, "Come on!" and Dorothy, always fired by such enthusiasm, soon had him squealing with delight as she pretended to give chase. He pattered along the corridor while she crept stealthily behind. When she tried to coax him to her, he giggled naughtily and his plump little legs ran faster. Thus challenged, she went after him with more determination and caught him up in her arms. He accepted her readily this time, for his nurse was scurrying towards them.

"Oh, madam, I'm so glad you found him," she said breathlessly.

"It's truer to say that he found me!" observed Dorothy.

"God bless the little man. He has an enterprising turn of mind."

Dorothy smiled at that and George beamed back at her angelically.

"He does not often go missing from you?" she queried the nurse.

"No, madam. This is the only time."

George began to show interest in the small ruff around his mother's neck.

"I would have him with me awhile," she told the nurse. "Come, let us go and find your papa."

Missing! The very idea of her baby going missing smote Dorothy with a pain that she could hardly mask. There was so much of her in this sunny-natured child, yet she hoped for his sake that he would have his father's strength of character.

John was looking out for her and on seeing him in that instant, she thought admiringly that he had certainly passed his physical robustness on to his son. He seemed so happy as he came towards her that for Dorothy, the years suddenly slid away to two young lovers who stood in each other's embrace on the little bridge at Haddon. The bridge – that had been the setting of her youthful dream about the future, *their* dream, and through the heights they had known together they had made much of it into reality. And would achieve much more ...

"I see now why you were delayed," he smiled, opening his arms out to her.

George interpreted this movement as meant for him and flapped out his arms at his father, straining forward as far as he could.

"Let me relieve you of your imp," John ventured.

"*My* imp?" grimaced Dorothy, her eyes twinkling as the transfer was successfully accomplished.

"All right, *our* imp!" he agreed, firmly extricating his nose from his son's over-zealous attention.

She was aware then that John watched her closely and she coloured under his scrutiny, and yet was glad of this, for she sensed his love come out to her, sensed that he had caught echoes from her mind.

"Dorothy, do you crave to be back in Derbyshire?" he asked.

"No, John. Not just yet."

"Are you sure?"

"Yes, quite sure." She met his gaze steadily. "That promise I made to you before we left Haddon, my will to keep it has now increased a hundredfold."

He smiled at her again and it seemed to her then that she had overcome some kind of crisis. A small one, but still enough to have affected her profoundly. She recollected that on her wedding day she had hoped always to try and preserve her happiness. And so she would. Never had she felt so certain. The ring-finger had worked its healing and with the ceasing of struggle, a feeling of ease had come to her such as she had not known before.

"I shall not be like the ..." she began to add with great feeling.

"Ssh!" John interrupted, grinning as he did so.

"Ssh!" spluttered George, putting his finger over his mouth in like manner.

Laughing, she realized that others may still be within earshot. She pressed her hand on John's shoulder. "I shall not be like the Queen of Scots," she whispered. "I will do nothing to risk being separated from my husband and my son."

Then happily they walked together back to their apartments, to the accompaniment of shushing noises along the corridor.

The Earl of Derby had an almost royal lifestyle. So magnificent were the feasting and revels at Lathom that Thomas seemed to be dancing on air. The letter was signed and soon it would be with Queen Mary. A true sense of destiny had he enjoyed since he signed that coded missive, added the name of his brother and then watched while Sir Thomas Gerard signed his.

The more cautious side of his nature tended to cast doubts about his fellow-conspirators. He hoped that Gerard would not be over-liberal in speech about the matter and so betray their plans, that Rolleston too would keep silent, especially from his son. A petulant youth in Thomas's view, and extremely untrustworthy.

As for John Hall, he had warned him to take the greatest
care. Hall was known to Shrewsbury and his servants. That
might work to the plotters' advantage or more easily bring their
downfall. It was a pity that Hall's dour and rather abrasive
manner had not endeared him to Thomas, nor the fact that he
had criticized his handwriting. But these were minor irritations.
So said Thomas's generous, forgiving traits. The letter was on
its way now and hope's magic gilded the summer hours for him
while he anticipated the Queen's reply.

On August 13th, the appointed moorland meeting was kept,
and on the next day, John Beaton returned to the moors to
deliver her answer to Hall.

"This is the last time I may leave Chatsworth for the purpose
of this plot," said Beaton.

"Are you under suspicion?"

"It is to avoid suspicion that I tell you this. If more secret
messages are needed, you must find another means of sending
them."

"The Queen's safety is our main concern at all times,"
agreed Hall.

"Indeed it is," stressed the Scotsman, handing him the sealed
packet. "Her Majesty's safety – and yours. For that reason, the
Queen, my mistress, is very much afraid of failure, Master Hall.
The damage to her cause could be irreparable. The
consequences for all who take part ..."

"We know full well the risks we run," retorted Hall. "We
dwell more on the glories of success!"

"Then go, man, at once. And I pray God you are not
intercepted."

But the glories of success were to prove a very distant
prospect on Hall's crucial return journey to Lathom.

He went first to Francis Rolleston's house, having arranged
to stay the night there.

"Well, where is it?" demanded Rolleston once the courtesies
of greeting were over.

Hall had the Queen's reply hidden inside his doublet and
almost grudgingly gave it to his host.

"Good man," congratulated Rolleston.

"Shall we open it?"

"I'll admit I am tempted to do so. But I believe that right belongs to Sir Thomas Stanley."

Hall put the letter away.

"By the way, my son has joined our select little band," said Rolleston. "Can we find some use for him?"

"Perhaps. Tis always best to have people in reserve," Hall replied. "How much does he know?"

"Very little, as yet. I thought we could tell him more tonight."

The two men moved into a mood of celebration and had already drunk a considerable quantity of wine by the time Rolleston's son swaggered in for supper. He was a pimpled, beardless youth, who was greeted by his father as "George, lad", and before long the stream of lewd jokes which he began was flowing almost as freely as the wine, each tale outdoing its predecessor for coarseness. He erupted into a bawdy song about Queen Elizabeth and her Court.

"The virgin Queen? Don't you believe it!" he declared, amid snide cheers of "God save the Queen".

"That's a good one. The best I've heard," slurred his father, splashing more wine into their goblets. The elder Rolleston seemed by now so befuddled that he splashed as much on the table.

"Where did you learn it?" asked Hall.

"From a friend of mine. The one who mewed my hawks." The son spoke loudly into his father's ear as if he was patronizing a backward child.

Francis Rolleston grunted, then swayed towards Hall and slapped him amicably on the shoulder. "Let's see the letter agin," he hiccuped.

Hall fumbled inside his doublet, muttering a little thickly and after a while placed the letter on the table.

George Rolleston, meanwhile, made much of drinking various toasts and afterwards refilling the wine-cups.

"More? Still more?" he kept enquiring. "Say when."

"When! When!" echoed the other two, between guffaws of laughter.

Hall blinked, his mind swerving back to a previous line of talk. He could not remember having put the letter away, but he had become so used to doing this now that he performed the task without thinking. Quite plainly, the letter was not on the table, so he must have concealed it again.

The Rollestons were grinning into their goblets over another jest made by the son, some kind of derogatory remark about the noble sport of hunting.

Hall, himself a keen huntsman, took immediate exception to this. "Well you may scoff," he bellowed, "but hunting is a far more manly sport than hawking."

George Rolleston reacted by taking a huge gulp of wine into his mouth and spitting it out on the rushes. A fierce argument then ensued about the merits of each sport, neither man able to convince the other but battling to provoke him further. The feeble attempts of Francis Rolleston to stop them went unheeded as the youth parried his opponent's verbal thrust by jeering with a vicious contempt.

"Scoffer!" Hall shrilled back at him, seeking the final word. "D'ye know what Solomon said of scoffers? Eh, lad? That they are an abomination to mankind!"

He gave a smirk of self-congratulation as he saw young Rolleston's jaw drop.

Hall's smugness, however, was to be very short-lived.

"Gentlemen," intervened his host again. "Now let us make friends."

"If this is your friend, father," said his son coldly, "then you shall be judged by the company you keep."

"What mean you, son? Explain yourself."

"So *this* is the man you chose to travel for you in connection with your plot."

"I am old. You know I cannot travel fast."

"Well, why didn't you ask me?" he glowered resentfully.

"Son, you have no right to question my decisions," blustered his father after a moment's hesitation.

"Oh no?" With a vengeful flourish of triumph, George Rolleston held aloft Queen Mary's letter. "I am sure this will make very interesting reading for the Lords of the Privy

Council," he cried.

Hall sprang up as if cold water had suddenly been dashed over him.

"One of our number?" he yelled at Francis Rolleston. "*One of our number!*"

"I am a loyal subject of Queen Elizabeth," said the youth.

"Take no notice," his father reassured Hall. "He's bluffing."

"Well, I'm taking no chances," said Hall, lurching round the table towards his quarry.

The young man jumped swiftly to his feet, knocking against the table as Hall lunged. A determined hand shot out and clamped itself over his wrist, while another tried to wrench the letter out of his grasp. They struggled, panting and cursing. George Rolleston reeled backwards under the onslaught of the stockier Hall, but recovering himself, attempted wildly with his free hand to snatch his knife from the table edge.

"Oh no, you don't!" screeched his father, desperately sweeping this out of reach.

That caused a fleeting lapse of concentration as the son reviled him with an oath. Hall's left hand let go its grip on the youth's wrist, while his sword hand locked rapidly into a solid fist. He hit George Rolleston squarely on his spotty chin and sent him tottering to the floor. And with a swipe at "Master Scoffer" 's hand, Hall took repossession of the letter.

"Go on, man! There is no point in tarrying," Francis Rolleston exhorted him.

"I will continue with our quest," Hall agreed, still gasping.

His fellow-conspirator nodded, ignoring the moans of his son as he picked himself up from the floor.

But the son's parting words stayed to haunt Hall for the rest of his journey: "I am a loyal subject of Queen Elizabeth. You have not heard the last of this!"

Thomas, in his boyish eagerness to continue with the adventure, did not comment on how Hall came to him with only a token air of cordiality.

His breathing quickened when he saw Queen Mary's letter.

"At last, at last!" he cried. "I'm in a fever to know what's in it."

He broke the seal and impatiently perused the contents.

"She gives her consent!" he said. "She says that no doubt the Kings of France and Spain will intercede for her with Queen Elizabeth, but when will that be? And we may restore her liberty long before!" He kissed the letter and pressed it to his heart. "Master Hall, we must find another way of getting messages into Chatsworth. I trust you can gain entry to the Shrewsbury household?"

"Aye," answered Hall tonelessly, and then, "Sir Thomas, there is something else you should know."

"Fire away, my friend!"

Hall hunched himself up nervously in his chair and related in detail his visit to Rolleston's house. All happiness died on Thomas's face; in his mind he had fallen to earth again and far, far below, down a dark and noisome chasm where the angry waves surged mercilessly to sweep him to his doom.

"Fools! God blast you!" he roared in anguish and dismay. "I believe young Rolleston will betray us all. We are undone before we've even started."

"Do not disturb yourself so," Hall rebuked him. "Maybe he doesn't know of your involvement in this. But of my part he does know ..."

"I would advise you to lay low," said Thomas.

"I have a cousin in Shropshire. I could go there for a while."

"Good. And this –" Thomas's attention turned once more to the letter and the royal captive's cipher. "This is the evidence against us and both must be destroyed!" His voice rose again in response to the fear and rage which so painfully gnawed at him. And he ripped and shredded both documents with all the thoroughness of a man who had hitherto borne most of life's sufferings with patience. He summoned his servant, ordered a fire to be lit and then cast every piece into the flames.

Later, Hall left Lathom for Shropshire.

A few days passed. Thomas sent for Francis Rolleston before he prepared for his own departure to Tong Castle.

He greeted this new guest reproachfully.

Rolleston sighed, acknowledging his mistake in telling his son. "Alas, these matters cause such disunity within families," he said. "How easily I can apologize in retrospect! I genuinely thought my son might be useful to us."

"Well, what now?"

"We must put aside our hopes for the time being."

"I don't need you to tell me that!"

"But take heart, Sir Thomas," Rolleston reassured him, "for neither you nor I are under any kind of suspicion. My dutiful son has seen to that," he added with a bitter note of irony.

Thomas hardly dared to ask, "Has he revealed the plot?"

"Aye, Judas that he is!"

"So soon?"

"I tried my utmost to stop him," Rolleston went on. "I told him that if he informed the Privy Council, they would ask him how he knew of it. And that would lead them to me. His own father! He agreed that he could not betray *me* and so I thought I had dissuaded him. Then I learnt from my servant that he had sent a note to London."

"The damned little rat!" interjected Thomas. "If he were my son ... sorry, please continue, my friend."

"Well, naturally I challenged him about the note and the insolent young scoundrel said that if he wasn't going to belong to this plot, neither was I. He had disclosed the matter to their lordships, named Hall and signed his letter, 'From a friend who does not conspire against Elizabeth, his lawful Queen'."

"An anonymous letter," observed Thomas in disgust.

"My son knew only of my part in the plot – and Hall's of course," said the older man. "He suggested that we forget about it now, but I pointed out to him that was impossible, since Hall would not take all the blame on himself if he were arrested. So then he replied that Hall is my problem – or rather, Sir Thomas, he is our problem. Remember, so long as he stays free, we are safe enough."

"So long as Hall stays free," mused Thomas, stroking his neatly bearded chin. "Master Rolleston, we must make sure that he stays free!"

Slowly, his fog of self-pity was lifting, allowing the sun to break through once more. They must devise some means whereby they could rid themselves of Hall, since the man was no longer their asset, but a liability and potential traitor to them.

And if Hall was out of the way, the plot could soon be revived. Thomas would await a suitable opportunity. He was too deeply involved to stop now.

The Great Bell of Tong Church was pealing its welcome over the Shropshire countryside. A Vernon had come to Tong. Dorothy, homeward bound with her husband and son now that August was nearing its close, had arrived here to see her sister. She had never failed to be moved by this village custom towards her family, and before she entered the castle gateway she turned round to glimpse once more the imposing red stone church where so many of her illustrious ancestors were buried. She was delighted to be here, delighted to be amongst her kinsfolk – whether past, present or future. A new life, she believed, was forming itself within her. Another child! The fruit of the new nearness between her and John.

So her family was now totally at the centre of her thoughts, diverting her attention away from matters more heavily strewn with pitfalls. This was no longer Dorothy the dreamer, the worried onlooker. This was Dorothy committed, absorbed and happy.

One morning, accompanied by her maid, she slipped away from the castle and walked past thatched cottages, through the green churchyard and into the shadowed nave. Joan remained silently at the back of the church, while Dorothy moved forward. She knelt beside the tomb of her grandparents and reached out to touch the small figure of her father, their only child. He was young there, without his long, pointed beard. Not as she remembered him! Her grandfather had died when George Vernon was only three. Her grandmother she could remember a little. The lady was tall and graceful, like Margaret, and she had married again – to John's uncle.

Their alabaster effigies shimmered in the dimness of the church. Here all were at peace, their images cast in brass or stone, their hands joined together in perpetual prayer. No more worries or cares to oppress them, no feverish hopes. Dorothy joined her own hands in prayer. She felt at one with her ancestors, these generations of Vernons who had lived so gloriously. Not one of them had fallen out of favour with their reigning monarchs, but stayed true to their family motto, DREDE GOD AND HONOR THE KYNG, those words carved, as if to remind her, above the fireplace of her much-loved parlour at Haddon.

"Dear Lord, would that I shall never let them down," she prayed. And she prayed too for the child she was carrying, for more children before her youth passed entirely away. She who had known such restless tumults in her early days did not regret to lose more of her wild impetuosity if now, still in the summer of her life, she could be sustained by her growing, sweet feeling of serenity.

With Joan she walked back slowly to the castle, gazing with pleasure at the scene around them – the octagonal church tower, cottages peeping through the trees, the outline of Welsh hills in the distance and the gentle, rippling stream which flowed into another near the castle.

A sudden soft breeze set the castle gardens in motion as they walked through, all except for one corner, the sunniest and most sheltered corner where roses climbed in great profusion against a high wall. Adjoining this, a thick wall held the doorway where they were heading.

"How beautifully those roses bloom," said Dorothy, stopping to survey them more leisurely.

Joan murmured her admiration. Then she curtsied and stepped behind again as a tall figure came towards them from the doorway.

"My Lord of Tong, we were praising your roses!" called Dorothy. And in a rustle of silken skirts, she went over the grass to meet Thomas. How handsome he looked as he smiled at her! So full of purpose. But why was he here at this moment? A chance encounter? She felt unwilling to signal Joan to leave them, for she had sensed since their arrival at Tong that Thomas wished to speak with her alone and she could guess what it might be about. Some way of helping Mary Queen of Scots? Some way of testing her promise to John!

She made no move to dismiss her maid. She saw Thomas's face grow serious. He studied her thoughtfully and told her, "Yes, the rose blooms fair and lovely."

She glanced once more at the wall and quickly back at Thomas. His eyes had not left her. There was an intensity about him which suddenly jolted her into acute remembrance of someone else, years ago, who had looked at her like that. And the pain of it made her want to recoil from him. Yes, Thomas did resemble his brother. She saw him just then not as her friend, but as a threat to her, a shadow across the brightness of her happiness. And she had so much to lose now.

Her inspiration came from that sunny corner. She gave him back look for look and said slowly and deliberately, "Small wonder these roses bloom so fair, for they are protected by a high wall."

Her eyes appealed to him for some sign of understanding, however faint. If she was the rose, then John was the high wall to shelter her. *Shelter*, not enclose her like a prison wall. She was not a winged creature who could soar towards the sun and even if she could, she would not risk flying too high only to plummet, scorched and screaming, back to earth.

With a half-sigh, Thomas conveyed to her that understanding. She smiled at him, relieved. He shrugged his shoulders in the light manner she had seen before. They talked about the weather. Thomas did not seek her alone again.

By early September, Dorothy and John were once more in residence at Haddon. It came as no surprise to them when, not long after their return, the Earl of Shrewsbury sent his messenger with an urgent request for their company.

Dorothy was shocked, however, when they were ushered into the Earl's presence at Chatsworth. Not because of their welcome, which was undeniably warm, even from the Countess. But how he had aged in the few short months since she saw him!

"Ah, it does my heart good to be with you again," he said, eyeing them both approvingly.

"Why not a little music to celebrate your homecoming?" added Bess.

The offer was joyfully accepted.

"Excellent," she cooed. "I suggested to the Queen of Scots that she should invite us to her apartments. Naturally, she agreed without hesitation."

Now it was Dorothy's turn to view Bess with approval. Astonishing, she thought, that once the inevitable is bravely faced, how quickly reluctance can turn to gladness. It was inevitable that she should be friends with Bess. How often had she told herself? No-one could doubt her ladyship's great organizing skills or that she was the best of company when decisions were entrusted to her.

Shrewsbury informed them, "You will not have us so near to you for much longer. Any day now I expect to receive instructions from London, saying that the Queen of Scots is to be removed from here forthwith. To Sheffield, I hope."

"But to spite us, it may be Tutbury." The Countess wrinkled her nose.

"Why can't she stay at Chatsworth?" asked John.

Dorothy held her breath. She believed she knew the answer already.

"There has been a plot to free her," the Earl confirmed.

"Have any arrests been made?"

"Not yet." There was a note of bitterness now in Shrewsbury's voice and a hint of that latent determination which Dorothy knew so well. "I seek for questioning John Hall, a former servant of mine. Doubtless there are others involved, but we shall not know who until he is captured. If you hear aught of his whereabouts, of course you will assist me."

"Of course," replied John. "But surely there are those among Queen Mary's household who co-operated with him?"

"There – *was*," explained the Earl.

"Was?"

"The chief suspect is dead, as luck would have it! Died of dysentery, much to Queen Mary's sorrow. John Beaton, the master of her household, no less. He was a faithful servant. She tells me she misses him greatly. But she would have lost his service anyway if complicity had been proved against him."

Bess made certain she had her say. "We were put on our guard when we heard her windows had been measured – so that she might climb through them and escape!"

Escape through her window? Dorothy and John smiled each other's thoughts, only Dorothy's ran on: Windows? Oh God, Thomas, no! Was that how you wanted me to help you? Perhaps she would never know. And truly, she did not wish to know!

"Ha!" continued Bess, exuberant at their outward response. "Who would want to leave my Chatsworth?"

Indeed, no-one in their senses. Suitable grunts and clucks were made to humour her, indulgent compliments about the grandeur of her home.

Now that she had begun, her sarcasm must run its course. "From her little bower, my lord, your precious Queen can see how difficult it is to escape from Chatsworth. The evidence is all around her! High hills of the Peak to hem her in, wild, barren moors for miles, and guards beneath her tower when she gazes despondently down. Only if she changed herself into a mouse or a flea might she escape!"

"The poor woman is ill," retorted Shrewsbury. "I doubt she has the strength to escape."

Bess regarded him with a stony air. He had silenced her, though she was clearly in charge again when she led them towards the Scottish Queen's apartments. Dorothy tried hard to cheer her. It was a simple task. She felt pleased, for her efforts enabled her to repress other, less congenial notions. If Thomas was a party to this plot, he might have brought her into it – if she had not been away from Derbyshire, if John had not guided her back to the right path … If, if! She recognized how useful she might have been to the plotters, how easily she could have acted as a go-between, slipping secret messages in and out of Chatsworth under ideal circumstances such as this musical gathering.

Her relief, her gratitude that this had not been allowed to happen, was something she could not express in words.

But her love for music she could express. Already, close

behind her, John was humming a tune, and she and the Countess joined in together.

"I trust you will favour us with a song, John," said the Earl.

"It would give me the greatest pleasure."

"Nay, that honour belongs to us."

Pleasure was very much the sentiment on Queen Mary's face when she proffered her own lute to John. "I'm told you are very gifted, Master Manners. I long to hear your music."

"Then by your leave, Your Majesty," replied John with all due deference to her rank, "I will sing for you in praise of music."

He began to play and his rich voice floated over the diverse audience:

> *Where griping griefs the heart would wound*
> *And doleful dumps the mind oppress*
> *There music with her silver sound*
> *With speed is wont to send redress*
> *Of troubled minds, for every sore*
> *Sweet music has a salve in store ...*

His silver notes did much to send redress to all the careworn minds who listened, and when he had finished, the warmest applause came from Mary herself. It was a touching scene, Dorothy thought with pride, to see her husband hand the lute back to this foreign Queen with whom he had so little in common. Every movement of his body and the carriage of his head showed obeisance while that of the Queen her obvious appreciation. A shared delight in music – momentarily it had brought these people together and made them forget their differences.

With all her heart in that instant, she wished that time would stand still. But it was not to be. Even as she understood fully the joy of this coming together, the moment was gone.

Mary played the lute herself and treated the company to songs of the French Court where she had been brought up. There was a wistfulness in her beautiful voice and she seemed to lavish affection on her lute, as though it were a living thing. Hers was clearly a generous nature much in need of affection, and sympathy.

But look where sympathy had brought many of her followers! Death, imprisonment, and other sufferings untold.

Thomas, if you or I had deserved imprisonment for partaking in that plot, we would not be kept in such state as this, Dorothy reflected.

So she guarded her sympathy, as she had learnt to do. But while the music continued, her attention focussed on the young page boy who was in attendance on Shrewsbury. And having noticed him particularly, she felt compelled to continue watching him. There was something in the child's bearing perhaps, his mannerisms, his sheer attractiveness which reminded her of Thomas and she judged him to be about the same age as her nephew.

"Anthony Babington," whispered Bess, who was seated next to her. She nodded towards the boy.

"Of course," smiled Dorothy. "The Babingtons of Dethick. Good Derbyshire family."

"Catholic," said Bess disapprovingly.

Catholic! *And* he has eyes only for the captive Queen, thought Dorothy, observing his expression. Eyes which showed the same adoring fanaticism as those of Thomas.

She turned her gaze slowly and imperceptibly away from him. He was only a child, she comforted herself. But she did not want to think what the future might hold for him.

The immediate future, however, held an incident for her to savour. When the music came to its close, Bess marshalled Dorothy aside to admire the tapestry which she and Mary were working.

Another shared delight!

"Why, it's charming. Exquisite," said Dorothy with all true sincerity.

"All day she plies with her needle till very pain makes her give it over," gossiped Bess.

"But the result is well worthwhile."

Bess inclined her head in the way she did when she was pleased. Dorothy grew a little less wary of her.

"It eases the tedium of her imprisonment," said the Countess.

Tedium. Boredom. That must be the worst aspect of her captivity. The Lady of Haddon restrained herself from mentioning this. The statement was made instead by the softly-spoken Queen.

"Yet any interruption of this boredom can be very disturbing," she added.

"Your Majesty does not find musical festivities disturbing?" enquired Dorothy, aware of Bess's indignation.

A slight smile appeared on Mary's sad face. "Music will ever be a balm to soothe my woes."

Bess reverted to her former expression.

Then Mary asked, "My lady, can you spare Mistress Manners for a few minutes? I would show her other examples of our needlework – *in private*."

The last words were uttered in the form of a command. She looked so regal standing beside the Countess that she was not to be denied. Though she had graciously acknowledged Bess's self-appointed position as head of the Shrewsbury entourage, everyone must bear in mind that only one life separated her from being in reality their Sovereign Lady. She may not always be a prisoner. And if her fortunes ever did change so dramatically as to make her the Queen of England, she would reserve her bounty for those who had dealt with her considerately in times of adversity.

Dorothy followed the royal captive into an adjoining room. Was this another crisis to test her? Maybe the Queen wished her to replace the late John Beaton as her secret messenger! Odd that Mary was disquieted by interference with her boredom when she had a reputation for thriving on intrigue.

A memory pierced Dorothy from the days of her own distress. It belonged to that time on the Isle of Man when she had seen the Scottish coast, a viewing filled with portent for her, though she did not realize its deep significance then. She had never envisaged finding herself in a situation such as this. But here she was, and seemingly without effort she collected herself to cope with it.

They talked at first of their sons in a deceptively breezy way. That the Queen of Scots was a gentle, loving woman was very plain. She was the kind with whom Dorothy could have made a lasting friendship, under better circumstances. But there must be no overflow of her affection along Mary's treacherous path.

"I am with child again, Your Majesty," she said meaningfully.

Mary clasped her hands in genuine delight.

"Then I will set to work on a gift for you," she replied.

The conversation drifted on to Mary's ostensible reason for bringing Dorothy here – to marvel at more tapestries. And marvel at them she did. There was one piece of especial interest. It depicted an armed man within a border of crosses. White diagonal crosses on a blue background.

"The cross of St Andrew," said Mary solemnly.

"Your Majesty, is this your father?" asked Dorothy, pointing to the initials I.V.S. beneath him.

"Yes, it is my father. King James V of Scotland." The Queen sighed, gazing at her hand-worked image of the father she had never known. "Dorothy, I would present this to you as a gift," she declared suddenly, "for the pleasure which your husband's music has given me today."

"Thank you."

"I have reason to be grateful to others of your close kin," Mary went on.

To whom was she referring? To Shrewsbury who was known to be a lenient jailer? Or to Thomas, who had once written secret letters to her and was maybe her would-be rescuer? Dorothy viewed the Queen's remark as a bait – and one imprudent enquiry from herself could be sufficient to ensnare her.

She stared at Mary impassively, determined this should stay unspoken.

"I will pray for you, Your Majesty," she said simply. "Please would you pray for me and the child I am to bear?"

Mary nodded. This was Dorothy's gift to her and she could hope for no more. Both in their individual ways were giving and receiving as a mark of mutual regard. The tapestry would be hung with great respect at Haddon.

Presently the two ladies went back to the outer chamber

where John and the Shrewsburys had lingered to wait for Dorothy.

They took their leave of the Queen with the customary courtesy, but as they returned to the Earl's apartments, it was John and not the Countess who walked along with Dorothy.

He drew her arm through his in a gesture so tender that she wanted to fling her arms around him there and then. She raised her brilliant eyes to him and saw the familiar, listening expression he always assumed when she had news to impart to him.

"Her Majesty of Scotland has seen fit to bestow a gift upon us," she said.

"For what purpose?"

"For that your music has given her much comfort to lighten her day."

"So," he grinned, "music will ever be my saving grace!"

FIFTEEN

Thomas remained high in his brother's esteem throughout the autumn and following winter. Not only because of the plot but also the way he had despatched John Hall along the escape route intended for the Queen of Scots – by ship to the Isle of Man and from there, to Scotland.

Hall took with him another secret letter, this one from Mary's envoy, the Bishop of Ross, to her staunchest supporters in her own realm.

So Thomas had not sent him away without purpose. The sense of destiny was still with Dorothy's brother-in-law, and that letter had drawn him into further intrigue, for he had received it in true cloak-and-dagger style one day from a complete stranger in London.

But while he had gained success in one direction, the weight of failure was heavy upon him. It was a constant source of regret that the matter had not proceeded far enough to attempt the actual rescue.

"If at first you don't succeed ..." Ned had reminded him.

Try, try again! That was what lay ahead of them this summer. Perhaps Mary would be back at Chatsworth by then. And even if she stayed at Sheffield, it was said that the manor house was relatively easy to escape from.

In May, Thomas took his wife and son to Haddon. The visit was necessary for business reasons, though it also provided a chance to see Dorothy before the birth of her child.

She was very relaxed in her advanced state of pregnancy. When she moved about, she did so carefully and she had, during these past months, developed an insatiable appetite for eggs. This craving of hers had caused consternation amongst her tenants and servants at first – most unsuitable fare for a lady, after all, even a lady in her condition!

But she had not lost her spirit, and encouraged by the mock disgust of Thomas and Margaret, she decided, during one of their meals, to shock them further by declaring, "Tis no worse than drinking the dried powder of earthworms in the broth of an ox's tongue."

"Ugh!" said Margaret.

Thomas was about to cram a piece of pigeon pie into his mouth, but appeared to change his mind.

"Why do you need to drink that?" he asked instead.

"I did not say that I drink it. Only I heard that it increases a mother's milk."

Thomas shook his head. "So, Mistress Doll, like the low-born you eat eggs and you would feed your baby yourself. Have you no wet nurse?"

The sisters eyed each other and giggled.

"John, I can assure you," smiled Margaret, "that your wife is in truth high-born, though to judge from her tastes ...!"

"The ways of women are always strange," John laughed, his eyes twinkling at Dorothy. He put his hands up to shield himself as she made pretence of hurling her trencher at him.

"It is perhaps as well that we dine privately in the parlour nowadays," observed Margaret.

The supper continued. Thomas consumed the pigeon pie

and had just begun work on a breast of roast partridge, when John informed them, "Lord Shrewsbury heard some good news today for once."

"Oh? What news was that?" asked Dorothy, aware that there was no flicker of interest from either Thomas or Margaret.

"John Hall has been captured in Scotland and handed over as a prisoner to England."

She cast him a sidelong glance. She wanted to say, "Don't talk about that. Let it rest," and he pressed her hand, indicating that he understood. But were his eyes really glinting at Thomas like chips of ice? She could not be certain. According to her knowledge, John had no reason to link Hall's name with that of Thomas Stanley.

Thomas himself, meanwhile, having shot a look at his wife and pushed his plate aside, forced some wine between his lips, which a moment later made him choke.

"What is it, my love? Your wine's too strong?" enquired Margaret, and he grunted, spluttering. "Let's mix more water with it then."

And she went on to do this efficiently, speaking all the while in a way which diverted the drift of conversation onto the carvings in the oak panelling.

She gazed round the room, declaring how much these all pleased her.

"Me too," added Dorothy with a desperate brightness, "especially old Henry VII over there."

Thomas gave a private look of thanks to Margaret as he received his wine back from her and encouraged Dorothy to enlarge upon the statement she had just made. Discussion moved on to consider the relative merits of the carvings above the fireplace and somehow the meal passed with everyone maintaining at least a semblance of normality.

Dorothy's glow of well-being closed round her again even before her sister and brother-in-law retired early, but gracefully, for the night. It seemed that Nature was determined to insulate her against the uncertainties outside, for although she could not walk far now before her body started to protest, she was totally at peace with herself and happy to exist from day to day, accepting wholeheartedly the burden which had so fortunately limited her horizons.

The next morning she ambled about the kitchen attending to household matters. What meats should be prepared for the day's meals, how many herbs and were there enough eggs and fish. It was Friday, but only Papists strictly observed the law which required abstinence from flesh meat.

She applied her own herbal remedy to the arm of a maid who had fallen, then dressed the wound of a forester injured during his work. Eventually, her back began to ache and she was forced to seek the comparative quiet of the parlour.

Already there she found Thomas and Margaret seated with their son in the oriel window recess. They greeted her with a certain detachment, a watching calmness from Margaret which did not soften when her sister sat opposite them.

"Thomas, is there aught I can do to help you?" asked Dorothy.

"Pray for me, Doll. There is nothing else you can do."

Pray for him, pray for this gloomy, fearful man who yesterday was vital Thomas! She was filled with pity at the sight of him. The swollen, bloodshot eyes, the pale face etched with a tinge of defiance, the arms rigidly folded to stop his hands from jittering. Suddenly Thomas had aged and yet there was something almost childlike about him. Dorothy knew then that her worst fears were confirmed. Thomas was a party to that plot. The sharp thrust of pain would once have overwhelmed her, stricken as she was also by the terrible realization that she was now in a possition to betray him.

Betray her sister's husband? In the past, both Thomas and Margaret had been an intrinsic part of her life. Yet in some ways she could feel that the past was over and done with and all that mattered to her was the future.

She looked towards Edward, thinking affectionately that for the future there was some hope. The boy would have come to her, but being older now was more reticent and adapted to the mood of his parents.

Her nephew was nearest the window. She swallowed, averted her gaze to her swollen belly and addressed herself to Thomas.

"A fine sight *I'd* make trying to escape through a window now! And in no way could I have helped another to do that."

He answered her kindly, without reproach, "Alas for me that I am not a rose and I have no high wall to protect me."

She sighed wistfully, "Oh Thomas, you had so much to live for ..." And her memory recalled vividly how years ago he had sought to help her in distress. She knew then that in her present situation, as with all the other important questions in her life, she must follow the urging of her heart.

But when her eyes took in Margaret, she felt sadness mixed with scorn. "Even now, must you appear so inscrutable?" she appealed to her. "The man you love will be taken from you. If I were you, I would that both these Queens and anyone else who caused this, might rot in Hell for all I cared."

Margaret responded with a faint, cool mockery. "Well, off you run. Go tell your Great Earl that the chief conspirator is here within his grasp. Arrest him now! And do not forget to display all the requisite embarrassment that one of your kin has dared to choose the losing side."

"You wrong me," flared Dorothy, and then the bitterness died in her as quickly as it came. "Ah, let it go."

She spilled on with more sympathy, "It is your tragedy that you have lost this time. But how can John or I be sure that we are on the winning side? As you have often said yourselves, the death of Elizabeth is all we need to turn our world completely over again and make your side the 'right' one."

Thomas gazed once more at the carving of Henry VII. "If only my family had not brought *you* to the throne," he jibed in frustration. "If only they had known what strife these Tudors arouse!"

And then Edward, his face flushed and pleading, asked Dorothy. "What will you do now?"

"I will pray for your father, as he requested," she said gently.

"And not tell of him?"

"I will never tell. How could I? But for the grace of God, I might have been going to prison with him."

At last there was a trace of emotion from Margaret. She raised a twisted hand to her mouth. "Aye," said Dorothy, noticing this, "I *would* have helped you, Thomas, had not fate led me to a wiser path."

It was honestly stated. Thomas seemed to regain some of his sparkle as he answered her, "I am glad for your sake that you didn't aid me."

"Dorothy, it was Thomas who arranged John Hall's escape to Scotland," said Margaret, her hands suddenly trembling uncontrollably in her lap.

Dorothy found she had gone to her sister – instinctively, just as her reluctance to betray Thomas was instinctive. She caught hold of Margaret's hands as if trying to pump strength back into her: another winged moment, yet its memory too would be a kind of holding. There were no tears, for Margaret recovered her composure quickly.

As Dorothy let go, she turned to Thomas again. "Then let justice take its course," she said woefully, "for John Hall and not John Manners will be your betrayer. But helping Hall, a wanted man, to flee, that will count as a further offence."

She went back to the opposite side of the recess. A fitting move. She had shown her goodwill as best she could and she did not feel guilty about keeping this from John, for she knew that he would not hesitate to arrest Thomas and convey him to the Earl, however painful that duty might be. With her influence, Dorothy hoped there would be less pain. John would find out anyway, soon enough, but Thomas and Margaret could be together for a little longer.

The division between Dorothy's family and Margaret's was made very plain at the midday meal, for the Stanleys ate no meat. How fortunate that she had a goodly variety of fish to offer.

"What was all that about?" asked John after their departure from Haddon. "Recusants?"

"It is their choice," she told him simply, and was glad he questioned her no further.

Dorothy had been walking into a storm along a castle wall-walk and stopped to gaze at a river. But the river, to her joy, turned out to be her beloved Wye at Haddon and the wall belonged to her bridge. And then a man had taken her by the hand and ridden away with her into the night, promising to love her always and shelter her from unhappiness.

She had borne him a son and now, within the birth-chamber, she heard the cry which brought her back to reality: she had given life to their second child.

"Oh, what is it?" she panted.

"A little girl," said the midwife.

"A girl?"

She raised her head to see the child, but someone renewed their mopping of her sweat-drenched brow.

"Give her to me," she demanded, thrusting away Joan's hands.

"Lady, you can have her, but first you must take your potion."

Dorothy groaned while her maid insisted on mopping her face once more. She then saw the midwife wrap her baby in a shawl and hand the tiny bundle to Joan, before coming forward with a draught for her. And in response she stretched her arms high up in the air and let them fall, slap, on the bed.

"I won't take it," she declared. "Not a drop until I hold my baby and my husband is brought to me."

"Headstrong, that's what you always were!" Joan remonstrated, trying to look stern.

But Dorothy pursed her lips in the way her first-born did when being dosed with food he did not approve of.

"Ah well," the midwife conceded with a smile. "I suppose your stubbornness is a good sign that you are none the worse for your ordeal."

Murmurs of delight rippled around the room. This had been a quicker and easier birth compared with the agony she had gone through for George. In her mind, Dorothy was prancing about with high steps of triumph, though her body was weak and spent.

That body had been cleansed by the time John came to her bedside. She lay with the baby in the crook of her arm, contentedly nuzzling the tiny, crumpled face.

He held her other hand and kissed it, then squeezed it with

tender amusement. "I heard the commotion you caused," he said.

"My conscience is clear," her pale, untroubled face pouted back at him. "John, is she not beautiful?"

He smiled agreement, but she wondered whether he did this solely to please her.

"Shall we name her Dorothy?" he suggested. "Gift of God?"

"No, I would rather call her Grace."

"Why so?"

"Because she, no less than you and our other babe, has been my saving grace." The *grace* of God which kept me safe from harm, her thoughts went on.

She believed she saw a glimmer of understanding as he gave his assent to that name. But this was neither the time nor the place to enlighten him further about remote and shady intrigues.

"You must rest now," he said gently.

"Yes, but stay close to me, John."

"I will."

"Everything is well – with us," she affirmed, and she made no attempt to remove her hand from his.

The weeks passed, halcyon days as Dorothy regained her health. Her looks were so far unimpaired by childbearing, though at twenty-six the slenderness of her extreme youth had softened into a rounded shapeliness.

George seemed somewhat puzzled by his new baby sister. Why couldn't she laugh and play with him? Why couldn't she speak? Why did she have no teeth?

The list of commands was endless from their nurse: don't breathe over her, don't poke sticky fingers in her face, don't make her cry ...

"All Grace does is sleep," he complained glumly one day to Dorothy, whom he was always glad to see.

An accurate observer, my little son! she thought. His description was as typical of Grace as John's comment of "forwardness" applied to George himself. Grace was a placid, undemanding child who rarely cried. George was inquisitive, outgoing and full of life. And Dorothy wished them no other way. She rejoiced to have two healthy children whom she and John loved dearly.

She was on her little bridge one afternoon in July when John's servant came to her, requesting her presence in the parlour. She followed him there immediately.

"I think you should read this," John said, offering a letter to her with an air of commiseration.

She took hold of this, noticing straight away the dreadful tidings contained in its midst: "Sir Thomas Stanley has been committed, a close prisoner, to the Tower for a conspiracy to convey away the Queen of Scots, to the further destruction of the State."

"Close prisoner," she repeated aloud. "The waste of it! Tis a cruel fate for such a generous man."

But because this bitter blow had been expected, Dorothy steeled herself against the churned-up feeling it inevitably evoked inside her and stood defiantly calm as she handed the letter back to John.

"You do not seem very surprised," he noted.

"Nor you."

"I must confess I had my suspicions, though never any real proof that Thomas had gone to such lengths."

"And if you had known, John, what would you have done? Informed on him?"

"I would have done my duty."

"I thought so."

"Dorothy, you knew about Thomas!" he cried with sudden fury.

"So?" she enquired flatly. "I kept my promise to you. I do not recall promising to inform on my friends."

"Did it not occur to you that the Isle of Man's Governor could sail to his island ,and escape almost anywhere from there?"

"Give him a little credit," Dorothy defended him sharply. "He understood that matters would go far worse for him if he tried to escape. So he waited, enjoying whatever was left to him of his freedom. Thomas never actually tried to get the Queen of

Scots out of Chatsworth. The whole framework of this plot seems to me very frail."

"Frail? I would say it has been disastrous for him. And even more disastrous for Lord Shrewsbury had it succeeded!"

"I do not condone his action," she said. "But I sympathize with him in that he was torn between two opposing loyalties. Thomas often found himself the middle-man between his two brothers. And now I, who have no brothers, understand that, for I have felt torn between two brothers-in-law. Both of them of conflicting allegiance and both of them good, kind men."

She stared at John then, boldly daring him to cross swords with her further. Roses have thorns, after all. But when he spoke again, his voice was touched by a new respect for her.

"We have both been caught in the middle, Dorothy, but you more so than I. And I believe you have conducted yourself with a loyalty, courage and compassion that I could never have shown."

For a moment Dorothy searched his face in surprise, then gently drew the letter out of his hand and placed it on the table. He caught her round the waist with an urgency to which her whole being responded. She pressed herself close to him in a silent rapture of relief that the storm for them was over.

Presently she said, "I am sorry for your sake, love, that we face acute embarrassment over this with the Shrewsburys. I can cope with that. Can you?"

"We both can."

He bent and kissed her to reassure her of their unity. Then he slackened his hold on her, but only slightly.

"How ... long do you think Thomas will stay in prison?" she asked.

"Two or three years, maybe. I cannot say. I'm afraid that its effect on him will probably last much longer."

Dorothy gave a deep sigh. "And my Lord Earl seems to have custody of the Queen of Scots indefinitely."

John tightened his arms around her once more as he said, "You know, that was a very wise judgement you made just over a year ago."

"A year ago? What did I say? For the life of me, I can't remember."

Eyes filled with love for her, he replied, "You said – 'How glad I am that we are not Thomas or Lord Shrewsbury. It is so much better to be us'."

Queen Mary presents a tapestry to Dorothy

PART V: 1576

'She – like some traveller who beholds the sun
Sinking before him ere his journey's done –
Regrets not now to lose its noontide power,
But hails the coolness of the evening hour.'

Agnes Strickland

Musical festivity with Mary Queen of Scots

SIXTEEN

The first coach ever to be seen in Derbyshire rumbled beneath the Peveril Tower and clattered to a halt in the upper courtyard at Haddon.

Dorothy, still convalescing after the birth of her fourth child, heard only too clearly the sounds of arrival, heard John shout his orders and then the thud of heavy riding boots as he ran up the stairs, probably two at a time she detected, towards their chamber.

He burst into the room, breathless with wonder.

"We can set off as soon as you are ready," he said. "The coach door is open and the steps are let down."

Dorothy curled herself up further on her settle. "John, you know I do not wish to go," she replied. "How can I leave you and the children, and all that is familiar to me?"

"Sweetheart," he said gently, "we have been through this already. The doctors insist you must take the waters at Buxton. Think of how my Lord Earl and Queen Mary herself have improved there! And she honours you be sending her own coach to convey you."

Dorothy nodded, sighing. Ah, if only I were well, she thought. But it was to make her well that she was going! Her loved ones feared they had lost her after this last baby, named John for his father. And John himself had spent days and nights on his knees praying for her recovery.

"Is it a handsome coach?" she asked.

"That's better!"

John smiled and went on to describe this novel mode of transport in the minutest detail, inside and out, even to an expert commendation of the team of fine horses which drew it. She managed a slight smile too, for he mentioned everything which Bess had told her, save for the royal arms of Scotland emblazoned on each door.

"Dorothy, where is your sense of adventure?" he continued.

"I thought you would embrace your first coach journey with open arms."

"Adventure?" Her face clouded again. "That so nearly brought me trouble. I prefer my life to be peaceful."

How could she explain to him? It was not that she had lost her irresistible urge for life, but this had channelled itself into a determined holding of their happiness. And they had been so happy. Well might John have sung, "Life, fly thou on" on the night of their elopement. The five years since Thomas's imprisonment had for the most part been kind to the Manners family of Haddon. It was true that her present health left much to be desired, true also that physical frailty was a problem she appeared to have passed to her youngest.

But what would life have been like for her if she had been forced to obey her father and marry Sir Edward Stanley thirteen years ago? Fines, and the constant threat of arrest for attending secret masses? She knew from her own experience how much the religious divide had worsened since that papal bull of 1570. "I think often of our last visit to Tong," she mused quietly.

"Of the Papist priest in disguise, do you mean?"

"Yes, John, amongst other things."

She had not dwelt on that, however, not knowing which of Thomas and Margaret's guests was a priest – only that her nephew had inadvertently referred to one of them as "Father" in her presence.

"Other things?" John prompted her.

"Thomas, as he is now," she said.

"I understand that, Dorothy," he replied. "It is not difficult for me to picture him either – so thin and wasted since his release from the Tower."

"And do you understand too, love, that I care nothing for queens and intrigues now that I have my own family to depend on me? Thomas was so – *alive*," she went on sadly, "but his confinement quenched all that. I do not fear to travel in this new and exciting way, only that return to a sense of ever-present danger which awaits me at journey's end."

John stooped down to cheer her. "'Tis not for long," he said.

Not for long! Her inner voice protested, for though she would be the welcome guest of Lord Shrewsbury, the Queen of Scots would also be at Buxton, enjoying more freedom than she did at Sheffield. And Dorothy would be almost alone there. Alone in that household of conspiracy! Thirty days the physicians had prescribed for her cure. Thirty days of using the baths and drinking St Ann's sacred water.

I will hasten back to Haddon before that time if I am healed, she assured herself convincingly.

John grinned at her, guessing the trend of her thoughts. She assumed her 'haughty' expression, playful and at the same time very coy. She would never quite lose that nature of following her impulses!

Footsteps and women's voices preceded a hesitant knock on the door. John rushed to open it and then Grace glided demurely in, closely followed by Joan and the nurse, Meg Needham, who was carrying the baby.

"I'm ready," Grace announced, flushing modestly with embarrassment as her father praised her attire.

She was a sturdily-built child, blue-eyed like her father and auburn-haired like her mother, and though she lacked Dorothy's slenderness, there was a resemblance in the litheness of her movements. Her gown of blue damask, exactly the same as her mother's, revealed a kirtle of amber beneath and trailed its fullness as she crossed over the chamber to stand by the settle. Fastidious in her appearance Grace was delighted at the prospect of actually being able to *travel* in her beautiful clothes and for Dorothy, the child's trusting need of her was a great comfort. Illness or no, she held herself responsible for her daughter's education and she was glad that Grace would be with her at Buxton.

The nurse also came forward and laid the baby in Dorothy's arms.

"So small and wan," Dorothy began to say. She loved him the more because he was so delicate.

"Many children are frail in their infancy," the nurse tried to reassure her, "and many of them grow out of it."

"Have a care of him, Meg," Dorothy admonished her gently.

"I will." She took hold of her tiny charge again and tears glistened her eyes. "Sweet lady," she snuffled, "do you come back to us healed."

Dorothy smiled, "I promise. And never yet have I broken a promise!"

Well-meant words, but when she was helped to her feet and had to be assisted by John down to the courtyard, Dorothy was keenly reminded of her weakness.

His arm was around her waist as he encouraged her towards the coach. William Crossland stood before it and bowed. He, along with John and the Queen of Scots' coachman, was to be her escort to Buxton. She glanced at the coach, bewildered. What a strange and heavy ... *thing* it was! She was thankful to turn her attention to the familiar again when she heard John mutter something to himself – a note of parental irritation.

"Where is Master George?" he demanded of his servants. "And even more to the point, what has he done with Roger?"

Grace stroked softly her mother's gown and pointed in her quiet, dependable way to the archway beneath the Peveril Tower. The head groom had appeared leading John's horse, Grey Haddon, while George walked, beaming with enthusiasm at the stallion's side. And perched somewhat precariously in the saddle was three year old Roger, who looked far from happy.

John muttered something stronger, then signalled to Joan to support her mistress while he strode purposefully across the courtyard and lifted his second son from the horse. The child tumbled gratefully into his arms and together, they went after George, though at a much slower pace than the headlong rush which he had made towards Dorothy. The boy lifted her spirits with his energetic account of how Roger had manfully ridden Grey Haddon all the way from the stables. And the groom, although he walked by the horse's head, only sometimes put his hand on the rein and he, George, had stayed all the time by the horse's side, but never once did he have to hold Roger's knee!

He paused for a brief moment, then added, "Mama, I wish we were travelling with you."

"Travel?" growled John, coming up to them at last. "Can

you talk of nothing else? You should attend first to your studies, my boy."

Having returned Roger, uncomplaining, to the ground, John shook his finger in mock disapproval at George and said, "Remember what we have told you."

"Yes, papa."

George drew himself up to his full height and folded his arms in the same way as his father.

"Two hours' hard study in the morning is better than four in the afternoon," he said mechanically.

"Good lad," John declared. "Even gallopers have to study, you know!"

Dorothy, meanwhile, found a grubby little hand had been thrust in hers when Roger came to stand quietly between her and Grace. She cast a smile in his direction, a placid smile, for he too was a sturdy little fellow, but in temperament akin to his sister. Perhaps, like her, he would be over-fond of his books when he was older. She could never imagine George as a scholar! But the finest horseman in the world or a traveller of great renown? Yes, she could picture him as these. George's first 'rides' had taken place on his father's shoulders, when he would ruffle the dark mane of hair and scream with the joy of it all – being swung up high in the air and carried with swiftness and ease. He would scream too when he was put down. Scream for more! Such memories made her delight to revel in her family and no doubt would serve to "undumpish" her, (as George would say) if she became too homesick at Buxton.

"Here's something for you, my love," said John, taking hold of her once more, "by courtesy of my Lord Earl."

George bowed solemnly before her, offering with trembling hands the stirrup-cup which she would normally give to John whenever he was about to leave Haddon.

She took it most graciously from him. "I thank you, young sir," she said.

Aware of her loved ones' eyes upon her, Dorothy drank deep from the cup. Slowly, a feeling of strength began to revive in her, thin as yet, but unmistakably full of promise. And the sweet taste of clear Buxton water lingered lightly on her tongue.

"Now you know it does you good," observed John.

"I shall drink it as much as I can."

Dorothy looked again at the coach, with more interest this time, in spite of herself. She could not stop her heart from lifting now to this setting out, helped in her acceptance of it by the warmth of her family around her and the reassuring knowledge that Buxton was not far away, being only some fourteen miles.

John began to lead her towards the coach.

"Would you prefer to sit facing the front," he asked, "and see where we are going? Or sit with your back to the coachman and see only where you have been?"

It seemed an appropriate question, not only concerning her journey, but also the present phase of her life.

"I will face the front," she decided.

She kissed a fond farewell to her sons, before being handed into the coach, and settling herself down at last derived even greater pleasure by watching Grace trying to emulate her. The little girl bestowed a kiss, gravely and sweetly, upon each brother, and not without encountering some protest, especially from George. Dorothy hoped for herself that she really would *see* where she was going. In the years already gone from her, tribulation had taught her to know her own failings, had taught her not to rush blindfold into potential danger. New challenges, maybe, she could not avoid, but it would be eyes and ears alert at Buxton!

SEVENTEEN

The month of July was almost over. The warm mineral baths were working their benefits upon her body, and it was Dorothy's delight to walk about unaided once more with all her former lightness of step.

She drank Buxton water with every meal. She joined in games of 'troll-my-dames', and when the weather was more agreeable, went down to the gardens to shoot at the archery butts. Without doubt, however, her most meaningful moments were those she spent with Grace. She had a daughter to be proud of. The child pleased everyone with her considerate and well-behaved manner, had settled into her new surroundings happily and made a friend of Bess's granddaughter, with whom she shared her lessons. Little Bessie Pierrepoint was god-daughter to the Queen of Scots and it seemed that Mary had been so long now with the Shrewsburys that she was almost part of the family.

But though the Earl's town house was pleasant and close, both to the baths and St Ann's Well, there were ills within his household which no amount of Buxton water would ever be able to cure.

People were in search of solace. Dorothy, with her cure nearing completion, looked forward to returning home. But others, she had found out since her arrival, consoled themselves in very different ways. And all the time she was learning, whether from her own or from other people's mistakes, how she could give of her best for her loved ones. It had been a long and sometimes difficult, winding road to achieve and then hold onto happiness. But having accomplished so much of her special dream, Dorothy was in search of its fulfilment.

The Countess had turned her business mind upon money-making schemes in order to finance her building programme at Chatsworth. She was already well-known for her acquisitive habits and had fallen into disagreement with the Earl for spending his money too freely.

But, in the words of Mary Queen of Scots, "Why be so rich when you have no-one to enrich?" And now Dorothy was discovering just how 'poor' Bess truly was in the midst of her material gain.

The advancing years had made little impression on her. Not even another spell of imprisonment in the Tower the previous year had dampened her high and ambitious spirit. Lord Shrewsbury had been outraged when, without their Sovereign's consent, Bess had married off her favourite daughter to a member of the blood royal. Queen Elizabeth was furious and immediately had her arrested. On her release, however, Bess had returned unrepentant to Derbyshire, hurling vindictive spite against her namesake Queen and at the same time exulting in the child of her daughter's royal marriage. For in this baby, Arabella Stuart, she, obscurely-born Bess of Hardwick, had a granddaughter in line for the throne!

It seemed that Bess was either unaware or totally unafraid of the extremes to which her ambition was capable of hurrying her. Not only had she angered and embarrassed her husband, but added even greater stress to his household. The Queen of Scots, seen now by Bess as a rival claimant for that coveted English throne, had been treated less kindly by her since the birth of Arabella.

But the Countess had paid for her triumph: while the Queen of Scots consoled herself with her religion, his lordship, it transpired, was enjoying a more worldly remedy ...

One morning Joan drew back her mistress's bed-curtains with an air of irrepressible excitement.

Dorothy blinked at first. The sunlight seemed so dazzling, but when her vision cleared she was soon wise to Joan's mood.

The maid handed her a draught of Buxton water and fussed busily around the room.

"Joan, what is it you know that I don't know?" asked Dorothy.

"Why, lady, nothing. Well – nothing you should worry your sweet head about."

"Jo-oan ..."

"Tush! This coverlet needs repairing. I'll see to it today."

"Mistress Lomas, I am not a child, you know!"

Joan tutted. Dorothy grinned, with a hint of mischief in her eyes, and said, "What's wrong? Are you pledged to secrecy or something?"

The maid answered with affected caution, "Well, I did promise I wouldn't tell."

"Nonsense! You can hardly contain yourself."

"Too true," laughed Joan. "But I know I can confide in you and trust you to keep a secret."

"An important secret?"

"Aye, madam. It concerns my Lord Earl."

Their faces immediately grew serious.

"I'm told he has a lover," Joan went on. "One of the serving-girls. A comely wench named Eleanor."

Without a flicker of surprise, Dorothy sighed, "'Tis sinful, I know, but I cannot say I blame him."

"It's all *her* fault," accused Joan. "Begging your pardon, madam, I mean my Lady Countess."

"Heaven help him if she finds out!"

"But she won't find out ... will she?"

"Not from me," affirmed Dorothy. "My sympathy is all with the Earl."

And with good reason, considered Dorothy, as Joan helped her to dress.

The friendship between John and the Earl had strengthened over the years, as John's power and prestige had grown in Derbyshire and Shrewsbury turned more and more to that rock-like quality in his character. The nearness of such a staunch ally helped the Earl to bear up under the strain of guarding the Queen of Scots. Dorothy admired now his foresight in applauding her marriage to John and sorely wished that he had been more fortunate with his own. She felt he deserved a better fate than this.

But Katherine, his much-mourned daughter, had been right when she said that the happiest part of him died with Gertrude. Life's sweet contentment still came to him, now and then, when he reminisced about her.

The Earl liked Dorothy to sit with him for a little while each evening.

"You are an excellent listener," he said to her that night. "I hope the ramblings of an old man do not bore you, Dorothy."

"On the contrary, my lord. I loved Lady Gertrude too, remember."

"Of course, my dear," he smiled. "Did you have a message from John today?"

"Yes, my lord."

"How fares my little godson?"

"I fear he is not as hale and hearty as his siblings," she replied.

"But that may change. All our children survived," reflected Shrewsbury, "almost all."

Then his face grew sad again, and Dorothy wondered whether he was thinking back to his wife's untimely death or grieving over Katherine's, or even for his "hasty" son, Gilbert, who was often at odds with him nowadays.

"I shall miss our talks when I return to Haddon," she said.

"I too," agreed the Earl. "But before you leave us, Dorothy, may I suggest an outing?"

"Where to?"

"I was thinking of Poole's Cavern. Tis not but a mile's ride from here."

"I believe that would invigorate us all," she said, and he nodded, but his face looked haggard in the gathering twilight.

She sensed that his friendship was reaching out to her. Not so much the subtle bond of rapport which she had always taken for granted. No, this was more like an appeal for help, for understanding and unswerving support – from her as well as John. Her kinsman was in need of good friends, now more so than in the past, and she committed herself to this need wholeheartedly. Nevertheless, the realization still seemed to her incredible that she, who had always leaned so heavily upon those closest to her, was now a shoulder upon whom others, of all ages, depended. The warm spontaneity of her nature was the quality which attracted and gave love, but time had taught her to control this, not to shed it, and so turn her lovingness into a triumph when it might so easily have led her to tragedy.

For Dorothy, the recent difficulties with her health made the ride to Poole's Cavern all the more exhilarating. The old temptation was still there, to spur her horse and gallop on ahead of her companions.

But now another girl with auburn hair sat before her in the saddle, and much of her enjoyment lay in witnessing her little daughter's interest in the changing scenes around them.

She endeavoured carefully to answer the child's ceaseless questions with honesty. They could not ignore the fact that the

Queen of Scots was with them, and she was surrounded by guards, or that the road leading out of Buxton seemed to be much frequented by beggars. However deeply she was attached to Grace, to all her children, she could not shield them from the world in which they lived. It was no less a dangerous place than it had been in her youth and somewhere inside her a voice was saying, "Do not love them too much, for one day they must leave you and take their places in this world. You cannot live their lives for them, only do your best to prepare them ..."

It sounded, curiously, like the resonant voice of her Uncle William Tailbois, and because she had always welcomed his advice, she felt certain it must be right.

The road twisted through rising pastures to the foot of Grin Low, where Poole's Cavern had its entrance. Suddenly, as the riders neared their destination, the trouble which followed Mary of Scotland like a permanent, haunting shadow once more made its presence felt.

Skulking in rags by the entrance to the cave was a group of beggars, who appeared to eye them malevolently. One of these, a boy, propelled himself forward and yelled at the top of his voice, "Gie us alms. Gie us alms, good Queen. We've naught to eat an' we've heard that ye're kind to the poor."

Mary raised her hand in acknowledgement, but before she could guide her horse nearer to the boy, Lord Shrewsbury's hand was upon her bridle. Guards closed in around her and evoked a rumble of discontent from the beggars.

"What are you afraid of, my lord?" she asked. "That by performing my small acts of charity, I shall endear myself to the people?"

Bess tittered scornfully. "More like repenting of her dissolute youth so as to ensure her a place in Heaven," she remarked, aside, to Dorothy.

In response she received a glance which neither agreed nor disagreed with her, for Dorothy's attention was elsewhere, intent upon the wearer of the little feathered hat in front of her.

"Please, mama," Grace had just asserted herself. "Please let us help these people."

But how? Dorothy affectionately adjusted her daughter's

cloak, for luckily an idea had come to her.

"My Lord Earl," she called out earnestly.

He looked round a little startled, but smiled kindly when he saw who wished to speak with him.

Mother and daughter rode forward and the guards parted to let them through.

"My lord," said Dorothy, "there is a way Her Majesty can aid these people without causing offence or danger. Let her pass to my child any money she wishes to give them, as I should like to do, and Mistress Grace can present this to yon lad."

"Very well," said Shrewsbury, letting go of the Queen's horse.

"Christ's blessings on you," said Mary, producing a handful of coins.

And Grace flushed modestly again, though she happily delivered the money into the boy's bony hands. More pleasure too was Dorothy's to know that Grace, while she was mostly biddable, clearly had a mind of her own.

The beggars were sent on their way and then the riders dismounted, following those guards who bore lighted torches into the darkness of the cave. Inside, the path was worn and slippery. The river Wye flowed through, for here was its source. Warnings were cried amid screams and giggles, and helping hands were offered to those unsure of their footing. Yet it seemed magical to be there in torchlight amongst the stalagmites and stalactites, and the animated faces of the company.

"We call that pillar Queen Mary's Pillar," the Earl told Dorothy. "So called on our last visit here."

Dorothy looked, admired and then turned her gaze on the river. "The Wye is so dark here," she noted, "but within a short distance it is delightfully clear."

"Does God live here?" Grace asked.

Her mother felt faint amusement. Grace always had such elevating thoughts! "God lives everywhere," was her answer.

But somehow Grace had decided that God lived in that cave. "One day, when I'm very big, I will walk all the way from home along by the river side and come and see God again," she informed them.

Shrewsbury patted her on the shoulder.

"There is something in what she says, you know. Life is like that – a journey along a river. Sometimes it is a raging torrent and other times it flows more smoothly, but hardly every slowly."

Dorothy agreed with him, though she concluded, "It is hard to imagine Grace every being carried along by a raging torrent! As for me, seeing this river in all its moods and seasons has been an endless fascination. I have found God further downstream as well as here."

"You are indeed blessed, my dear."

"Aye, my lord. God has been good to us."

He thanked her for the presence of mind she had shown in dealing with the beggars, and soon they returned to Buxton.

On the day when John came to escort her back to Haddon, Dorothy felt like the young girl again going to meet her lover. She had taken pains with her appearance. The riding habit became her well enough, but it was the glow about her which he remarked upon. That glow which made the whole world seem to sparkle with her, reflecting her joy with life in general.

"No need for you to travel by coach this time!" he smiled. "But you may have one of your own if you wish."

"Nay," she replied. "We are rich enough already." And then glancing at Grace, she continued, "Let's give the cost of a coach to the poor."

Their way home led through countryside both wild and picturesque, some of it part of their own estates.

How good to be going back, reflected Dorothy. Back to their world. Soon would be the busiest time of year on their lands – the harvest. Yet the life of a country lady may seen a passive existence to some, monotonous even. She thought of other words to counter this – fruitful, secure, acceptable – and all the more treasured by her because it was so dear-bought.

They crossed over the river Wye at Bakewell, stopping briefly while John cast a smooth, round stone into the water, "For luck," he said. They watched it skim two, three times across the surface, breaking the water into beauteous ripples before finally sinking.

With the memory of that sight to delight her eyes and the

murmur of the river still soothing her ears, Dorothy rode on home to her family, feeling ever more grateful for her blessings.

AFTERWORD

For the rest of Dorothy's life, the Manners family of Haddon enjoyed continued prosperity. In 1580 John was appointed Custos Rostulorum for Derbyshire and, as the marriage between the Earl and Countess of Shrewsbury irretrievably broke down, the Earl came to rely even more on his support.

Mary Queen of Scots was finally removed from Shrewsbury's custody in September 1584. In January of the following year her new jailer, Sir Ralph Sadler, summoned John Manners to attend upon her as she was taken from Wingfield Manor to Tutbury. From then onwards, her imprisonment became increasingly rigorous. She was at Chartley in 1586 when her last jailer, Sir Amyas Paulet, wrote four secret letters to John about her intended removal to Fotheringhay Castle in Northamptonshire. There she suffered trial and execution for her involvement in the Babington Plot. Anthony Babington, then a handsome young man of 25, was also executed. His plot, more far-reaching than the Stanley Plot of 1570, aimed not only to free Mary but also assassinate Elizabeth and place Mary on the throne instead.

Dorothy herself did not live to know of Mary's tragic end, for sadly she died in June 1584, aged 39. Like her parents, Dorothy was buried in the Vernon Chapel at Bakewell. John outlived her by almost twenty-seven years. He never remarried. He was knighted in 1603 and when he died in 1611, he was buried with Dorothy in the tomb he had erected to their memory.

Sir Thomas Stanley died in December 1576 at Tong, where he is buried. Margaret remarried in 1579, but when she died seventeen years later she was, at her own request, buried beside her first husband.

Of Thomas's younger brother, Sir Edward Stanley, it is said

that he so far forgot his duty to Queen Elizabeth as to take up arms against her in favour of Catholic Spain, where he was obliged to flee and died in exile and disgrace.

In contrast, Dorothy's stepmother, Maud, lived out her life happily. She died in 1596, still childless, but having enjoyed almost thirty years of the marriage she 'made by her own choice'. Although there is an effigy of her on Sir George Vernon's tomb at Bakewell, she is actually buried in Somerset.

In 1841, during restoration work at Bakewell, the bodies of Dorothy and John were found to be in a good state of preservation. Dorothy's auburn hair was still long and remarkably soft. Their third son, John, was buried with them. He died in 1590, aged 14.

Their other three children all survived to adulthood. Roger never married, but George did eventually settle down and marry Bess of Hardwick's granddaughter, Grace Pierrepoint. He lived at Aylestone until his father's death, then succeeded as Lord of Haddon. George's eldest son became the 8th Earl of Rutland and because of this, Haddon Hall is still owned today by Dorothy and John's direct descendants, the Dukes of Rutland.

Their daughter, Grace, married Sir Francis Fortescue of Salden, Buckinghamshire, and bore him thirteen children. In 1599 a Catholic priest arrived at Salden in disguise. He was the son of Sir Thomas Gerard and under his guidance, Grace was secretly converted to Catholicism. Father John Gerard described her in his autobiography as a remarkably modest woman for whom he set a high standard to live up to. She was obviously on friendly terms with her Catholic cousin, Edward Stanley, for her eldest son married one of his daughters. And so this marriage between Dorothy's grandson and Margaret's granddaughter re-united in the third generation the divided families of the two Vernon sisters.

Dorothy and Margaret discussing Thomas Stanley's active sympathy
for the cause of Mary Queen of Scots